"I asked out Katie Wing," Paul whispered. "And she said yes."

"Wow!" I exclaimed, surprised. "I can't believe you didn't tell me you liked her!"

"I didn't want to jinx it by saying anything," he replied.

Paul was actually interested in another girl. This was the first time in nearly a year that he'd asked out anyone. I darted a glance at him; he had a totally blissful look on his face.

So this was really great, right? Paul would date Katie, they'd fall madly in love, and maybe Frank would finally notice me and we'd become this major couple. Both Paul and I would be really happy, and we'd definitely still be the same best friends. Maybe we could even double-date.

Katie Wing, huh? She didn't exactly seem to be Paul's type—kind of flighty, and very girlie. But so what? *I'm sure she's nice if Paul likes her,* I thought happily. *And I'm glad he's moving on.* That was definitely a good thing. I *wanted* him to like someone else, didn't I? And now that he did, there was nothing holding me—or my heart—back.

His Other Girlfriend

LIESA ABRAMS

BANTAM BOOKS
NEW YORK · TORONTO · LONDON · SYDNEY · AUCKLAND

RL 6, age 12 and up

HIS OTHER GIRLFRIEND
A Bantam Book / January 2000

Cover photography by Michael Segal.

 Produced by 17th Street Productions, Inc.
33 West 17th Street
New York, NY 10011.

ISBN: 0-553-49295-0

Published simultaneously in the United States and Canada

Bantam Books are published by Bantam Books, a division of Random House, Inc. Its trademark, consisting of the words "Bantam Books" and the portrayal of a rooster, is Registered in U.S. Patent and Trademark Office and in other countries. Marca Registrada. Bantam Books, 1540 Broadway, New York, New York 10036.

PRINTED IN THE UNITED STATES OF AMERICA

OPM   0 9 8 7 6 5 4 3 2 1

To Arien, for always understanding. To Rosita, Dara, and Frank, for hanging in there through everything.

And especially to my grandparents, for all their support.

Prologue

September

"YOU'D BETTER MAKE this good for your little cheering squad." I grinned at Paul, tilting my head in the direction of the giggly girls bowling in the lane next to us. Could they have drooled over him any more?

"Whatever," Paul muttered, his cheeks slightly pink. I didn't know which amused me more—girls who ogled my best friend as though he were *YM*'s Hunk of the Year, or the way he barely seemed to notice.

I shifted around on my seat, hoping *I* didn't act like those girls around Frank London without realizing it. You knew when you were mooning over some guy, didn't you? Those giggly girls *knew* they were being totally obvious. As much as the sight of Frank turned my brain and knees to mush, I tried very hard not to show it.

Which was why he had no idea I had a huge crush on him.

"Watch and learn, Erica," Paul announced as he waited for his ball to be returned. "I'm gonna cream you."

Yeah, I thought. *Watch and learn how girls make total fools of themselves.* I glanced at the girls in Paul's cheering squad—they were staring and giggling and whispering. Why weren't they embarrassed to be so open about it?

Why did *I* have to be? At this rate, Frank would never know how much I liked him. Did I want him to? Yes. No. Yes.

No.

But what if there was a minuscule chance he'd be psyched to know I had a crush on him? What if he'd ask me out? *Yeah, right. Keep dreaming, Erica. The guy is out of your league.*

Paul shoved the sleeves of his dark blue sweatshirt up to his elbows as he reached down to pick up his ball. Our ogling neighbors were mesmerized by his forearms. He sent the ball down the lane, and I watched it curve to the right a little, then hit the two pin dead on. The pin teetered for a second, then spun and took the remaining one down with it.

"Ha!" Paul said triumphantly. The cheering squad whooped and clapped; Paul directed an embarrassed smile their way without really looking at them, then plopped down in the seat next to me.

"I still have one more chance to beat you,

Garabo." I jumped up and marched over to the lane. The gigglers gave me a bored look, then scrambled to their seats to gaze at Paul.

Who needs you guys? I told them silently. *I have my own personal cheering squad in my best friend. Even though he wants to win.*

That was what best friends were for.

I pushed my straight black hair behind my ears and picked up my ball, a red seven-pounder that Paul had given me a year before for my fourteenth birthday. I sent the ball toward the pins with a burst of speed, then turned to watch Paul's face and listen for the satisfying crash of a strike, which followed momentarily.

"Lucky shot," he said, grinning at me again. No whooping or clapping from his cheering squad.

My next ball landed in the gutter, and as soon as Paul stopped gloating about my lame finale and his win, we headed over to the sign-in desk to return our shoes. I glanced back at Paul's groupies; their necks were craned to get a good view of his butt.

Man! I knew the guy was incredibly cute, but give me a break! I guess when someone's your best friend and you don't feel *that* way about him, it's hard to imagine yourself ever checking out his Levi's.

Now Frank's, on the other hand . . .

Paul and I placed our bowling shoes on the desk and waited for the clerk to find our sneakers.

"Ew!" I almost shrieked, my attention caught by

a couple leaning against a video machine. "Check them out—that's totally gross!"

Paul turned and eyed the guy and girl who were all over each other. The girl had the guy pressed against the machine; his lips were attached to her neck, her hands somewhere in his thick hair.

"So?" Paul said, turning back to me. "They're in love. What's so gross about that?"

"Hel-lo? It's *sickening.*" Public displays of affection, otherwise known as PDAs, grossed me out. Why did couples think everyone wanted to watch them slurping each other?

Paul elbowed me in the ribs with a grin. "You're too private, Park. How do you think you show someone how much you like them? By keeping your hands off them?"

I rolled my eyes and was about to come back with some scathing comment, but Paul was staring down at the floor with a weird expression.

"Paul?" I said. "What's up?"

His head shot up as the clerk thunked our shoes on the desk. "Nothing. C'mon, Ms. I-Hate-PDAs." We passed the kissing couple on the way to the snack bar; they were now staring dreamily at each other, their hands entwined. I thought I might throw up.

Some things are meant to be personal. It's not like I have anything against a kiss here and there, or holding hands, but two people glued together in front of everyone is way too much.

"I just think that kind of stuff should be

between the two people, and not everyone else," I explained to Paul as we sat down at the snack bar counter. "Who needs to see all that gush and mush? It's gross."

Paul slid his knapsack under his stool. "If *you* felt that way about someone, you wouldn't think it was gross." We breathed in the delicious smell of greasy hamburgers and the snack bar's famous long, skinny fries. "I'm starving," he added. "Letting you almost win took a lot out of me."

I swatted his arm and laughed, but he was definitely wrong, wasn't he? I mean, there I was, dying over Frank London, and I couldn't imagine wanting to be pressed with him against a video machine at the Bowl-a-Rama. Was I the Martian, or was everyone else? PDAs were all over our high school. You couldn't walk down the hall without seeing someone's relationship acted out in front of you.

"Hey, Lee," Paul called out. "We'll have the usual."

The heavyset man at the soda machine turned to grin at us. "Coming right up," he promised, heading to the vat of french fries. Fifty-something Lee McKean had worked at the Bowl-a-Rama in Pikesville for as long as Paul and I had been coming, which was forever and all the time. Whenever Lee was having a slow day he'd listen to us ramble about our totally uneventful lives.

But my life *might* not be uneventful for long. One of my dreams had finally come true: I was now on the staff of the *Postscript*. And that meant my other dream had a slight chance of coming true too, since I'd be working with Frank London all the time! I still couldn't believe I was finally a sophomore and eligible to join the school newspaper. Journalism was great—it was all *facts*. Black and white. Who, what, when, where, why, and how. Stuff that was very easy to understand.

It was all the gray stuff in between that I had trouble with. Like what to do about making Frank notice me. There were no who-what-where-when-why-how guidelines about that.

Lee set down a large order of fries with Old Bay crab seasoning sprinkled on top, and Paul and I happily gorged ourselves. Stuffing my face helped take my mind off Frank. How gorgeous he was. How tall he was. How smart he was. How into being a journalist he was. He was the smartest guy in the sophomore class, and deputy to the two commentary editors, who were both juniors. That meant he'd definitely get the post the next year, and it was the most prestigious, important job on the paper.

"I wonder what my first assignment for the paper will be," I said, popping a fry into my mouth. I couldn't believe that the guy who made my heart feel all weird was into the same thing I was. The same passion! How cool was that?

Paul grinned at me. "Like you've talked about anything *but* the *Postscript* since you joined last week."

"I can't help it," I said, reaching for a wad of napkins. "You know how badly I wanted this. It's a *major* deal for me!" Freshmen were allowed to contribute articles to the paper, but only sophomores and up could join the staff. Erica Park, editorial assistant, Emerson High *Postscript*!

"You're so into it anybody'd think Ricky Martin worked for the paper too," Paul joked. "Not that *you'd* ever moon over some celebrity. You'd never moon over anyone."

I concentrated on taking a long sip of my Coke. I'd never told Paul about my crush on Frank. I'd liked Frank ever since I saw him for the first time, late the previous spring when he'd moved to Pikesville and started at Emerson. But the crush turned huge once I started reading his articles for the *Postscript*. He was so smart! So full of journalistic integrity! He wrote about important subjects that affected Emerson and Pikesville. He was serious, dedicated, passionate . . .

What would it be like to have some of that passion directed toward me?

I was willing to bet Frank London would never slurp some girl's face in public. I was willing to bet we saw eye to eye on lots of things.

So why had I never told my best friend that I was crazy about this guy? Granted, there had been only two months of school left when Frank transferred, and I didn't see him all summer. I'd figured I'd be over my crush by the time sophomore year began.

But I wasn't. In fact, it was bigger. He was taller. Broader. Blonder.

So was I just afraid to say it out loud to Paul? Afraid of letting *anyone* know, most of all Frank himself? Why did I have to be like this?

Paul had been my best friend forever. I could trust him totally. And now that sophomore year had started and I'd be working side by side with Frank, drooling inwardly, how could I keep it to myself? I had to tell Paul. He'd probably have great advice! Maybe I'd even tell my two other good friends, Linda and Sharon, and swear them to secrecy.

"You're not, um, totally off base about that Ricky Martin thing," I said, darting a glance at him.

He turned and stared at me, then grabbed a ketchup bottle, turned it upside down over the fry plate, and started squeezing. "Yeah . . . ?" he prompted.

"There's this guy, he's a sophomore too—an assistant editor," I blurted out. "I've sort of had a crush on him for a little while, but he wasn't in any of my classes last year, so I never had any reason to talk to him. I guess I could've told him how much I liked his articles or something, but I don't know . . . I thought he'd see right through me, you know? Like he'd instantly be able to tell how I felt."

I glanced at Paul; he was looking at me with a strange expression. "Sorry," I said. "It must be weird to hear all this when you didn't even know, and then I just gush the whole thing out in one breath!" I laughed. "I was embarrassed to tell you, I think. Because I'm probably not gonna do anything about it. Do you think that's totally lame?"

"It's not lame. It's normal." Paul paused in mid-motion, and ketchup dripped slowly out of the bottle onto our plate. "So why aren't you gonna go for it?"

That he wasn't mad at me for keeping it a secret was like a green light, and I grabbed his hands. I could feel my eyes twinkling, my face glowing. "I don't know. I mean, I guess I'm hoping for some kind of sign first. Paul, it was *incredible*. Last week, at my first meeting . . . I couldn't take my eyes off him! He's so cute, and he's so impressive! At the end of the meeting I finally worked up the guts to say something to him, an idea for an article. And he actually said it had some merit!"

Paul took a sip of his drink. "*That* was big of him," he said sarcastically, raising an eyebrow at me. "So who is he?"

"I know I probably don't have a chance." I frowned, swishing a fry in a dollop of ketchup. "I don't think he has a girlfriend, but I feel so *ordinary* around him. He's an assistant editor because he's so great at writing and editing. I'm just an editorial assistant. And he's so good-looking, and—"

"Did the captain of the football team suddenly turn academic and join the paper or something? Who *is* this guy?"

"Frank London," I said on a breath, closing my eyes for a second as his blond hair, green eyes, and broad shoulders floated into my mind.

I opened my eyes to find Paul staring at me, his mouth hanging open.

"*Frank London?*" he repeated, as though I'd just

announced I had a crush on Frankenstein's monster. "You've got to be kidding! He's so obnoxious! He was in a couple of my classes last year, and now I'm stuck with him on the yearbook committee. He's such a jerk, Erica. He transferred here six weeks before the end of school and acted like he ruled."

Now it was my turn to stare at Paul, mouth open. *Frank London?* The most amazing guy on the planet? "You must have caught him on a bad day or something, Paul." I turned back to the plate of fries, anger rushing up in me. This was just great. I finally work up the nerve to tell my best friend how much I like this guy, and he says Frank's a jerk!

Paul shook his head. "No, he's *always* obnoxious. He's definitely not worth obsessing over. And not . . . not worth you." He shrugged. "You deserve better. Besides, I don't even think the guy has any friends—that's how arrogant he is."

"I'm sure he has friends," I shot back, though I'd never really seen him hanging out with anyone. But there was nothing wrong with that. And if he didn't have a lot in common with the average sophomore guy, that wasn't exactly a bad thing. "And he is *so* smart, Paul," I added. "I think you're wrong about him. But it doesn't matter, because he'd never go for me anyway. I'm not exactly Ms. Hot or anything."

Paul's face softened. "Erica, you're—"

"*I'm* not the one who has every member of the opposite sex throwing themselves at my feet." I shook my head and stared at my glass. "So let's just forget it, okay? I'm sorry I mentioned it."

"Erica—"

"You know," I said, cutting him off, "I don't even get why you don't take advantage of all the attention. Do you realize how many girls have asked me to hook them up with you? If *you* had a crush on a girl, you'd have no problem letting her know and no problem getting her. You don't know what it's like."

Paul's olive-tinged cheeks were red. I studied him for a second, taking in those broad shoulders, that dark hair, those warm eyes that had girls swooning all over themselves. Anyone could see he was gorgeous—but I'd been looking into those eyes since I was five years old. I was immune. We were buds, and I guess I just never looked at Paul any other way. You knew when you felt major stuff for someone—the way I felt about Frank. With Paul it was like being with someone totally comfortable and familiar. Like a *brother*.

"Maybe I *do* know what it's like," Paul said, more to the french fry he was holding than to me.

"Huh?" Had Paul been harboring a secret crush on someone too? He rarely dated. I'd always thought he was just focused on school and lacrosse and the yearbook committee. But maybe he was too shy about going after the person he liked also.

Suddenly I felt so relieved. Paul and I could have been talking about this all spring and summer! We could have commiserated, compared notes. Instead, we'd both kept our mouths shut like idiots.

"Is it Karen?" I prompted. "From your English

11

class?" She was a thin girl with curly dark hair. I'd noticed her staring at Paul a lot.

Paul dropped the french fry on the plate and looked at me. Uneasily. "It's not Karen."

"Then who?" I asked, dying to know. What girl had finally gotten to Paul?

"Do you guys need a refill?" Lee interrupted, glancing from me to Paul and back again. He usually didn't encounter us acting so serious.

"No, we're fine," I said quickly. Lee shrugged and left us alone again.

Paul stared down at the counter as if the familiar yellow design were suddenly mesmerizing. "Look, just drop it, okay? It doesn't matter now anyway."

"Huh? Why? Does she have a boyfriend?" *Who is she?* I wondered, mentally flicking through the previous year's yearbook photos.

"Erica—" Paul lifted his head and looked at me. It was as though he was in incredible torment or something. Maybe this girl was just way out of his reach, the way I thought Frank was out of mine. But there was something else in Paul's expression— almost the way people looked at each other in movies when they were madly in love but too afraid to confess how they felt and—

Omigod.

Omigod. Omigod. Omigod.

I froze, except my heart was suddenly beating a million times a minute. I turned away, looking down, not knowing what to say, what to do. *Omigod. Omigod.*

12

He means me.

"So now you know," he said quietly. Even out of the corner of my eye I could see how tense his shoulders were. How tight his jaw was.

I swallowed.

Paul grimaced. "I'm sorry."

I didn't know what to say. What *do* you say when your best friend tells you after a hundred years that the girl he wants is *you?*

"Um, I—um, Paul, I—"

I suddenly felt dizzy, as though I'd have fallen right off the stool if my hands hadn't been braced on the counter. *How is this possible?* I wondered. *How could Paul like me that way? I'm Erica Park, his best bud. I saw him in his underwear when he was five. I saw him bawling when he was six. I saw him barf up his guts when he was ten and got food poisoning. He's my best friend. He's not a guy guy, and I'm not a girl girl.*

But now he was saying I was.

"But you like Frank." He leaned back on the stool. "I can't even believe I told you."

Omigod. Omigod.

"Paul, you're my best friend in the world. I, I—"

He let out a long breath, then braced his elbows on the counter and ran a hand through his hair.

"I like you, but not like that," I whispered.

Paul took another deep breath. "Look, you liking Frank London sort of made me sick, and if I didn't tell you how I, well . . ."

"I never thought of you like that," I stumbled,

keeping my eyes on the floor. "Like how I feel about Frank," I added, not knowing what else to say.

Paul straightened up. "Yeah, well . . ." he trailed off. "Can't say I blame you. After all, you did see me when I was covered head to toe with chicken pox. Remember how everyone called me Pizza-Face?"

I giggled, the mood lightened. "Yeah." Then I picked up a soggy fry and threw it at him. "Is this gonna mess things up with us? You're my best friend. I couldn't imagine not—"

"Don't worry," he said, turning to face me. "At least we have no secrets now, right?" He sent me a weak smile. "Maybe it's just a little crush, or maybe I just got jealous about Frank. No big deal, Erica, really."

"So we're okay?" I asked, relieved.

"We're okay," he told me, his smile more real now.

But were we?

One

February

WHY DID I have to pick today *to be a drab day?* I moaned inwardly as I hurried down the hall to the *Postscript* office. I glanced down at my faded jeans and baggy sweatshirt. If only I lived next door to the high school like my friend Linda Hitchen, I could have run home and changed.

It just figured that Mr. Serson would announce an emergency meeting for the paper's staff today. I'd spent the past four months trying to get Frank's attention, and showing up looking like this wasn't exactly going to help.

A quick scan through the tiny office's window revealed that he hadn't arrived yet. *Whew.* I pulled open the door and headed for the back of the room, sinking into the chair next to Linda's.

She looked me up and down, then raised her eyebrows. "Someone wasn't expecting to run into a certain someone else today," she singsonged, her catlike amber eyes twinkling. "I'm guessing this is a drab day?"

"Yeah," I answered, flinching. "Wonderful timing, right? Of course, it *would've* been if we'd had our meeting *tomorrow,* like we were supposed to."

Drab days had been Linda's idea from freshman year. When you were sure you wouldn't run into the guy you liked, you picked that day to look like whatever. Comfy clothes, like sweats or baggy jeans. Hair in a boring ponytail. Zippo makeup. Then, the next day, when you were sure you would run into the guy (or engineered it), you put on something you felt really good in, did something with your hair, whisked on the lip gloss and mascara and your mom's expensive perfume. The contrast between the days helped make you feel more attractive.

Not that I ever felt attractive, since I wasn't exactly a glamour girl. But the day after drab day did always help.

Linda shook her head. "That's gotta hurt," she said. "You-know-who should be here any second."

"You'd think I'd have learned from last year's drab day disaster, right?"

She laughed. "What, the day freshman pictures were announced as a fun surprise on our all-time drabbiest day?"

"Do I look totally awful?" I asked, checking if any loose strands of hair had sprung out of my ponytail.

"You look adorable as always," she assured me.

16

Yeah, right, I thought. *She's my friend. Of course she'll say that!*

I'd told Linda and our other good friend Sharon about my crush on Frank a few weeks after Paul had confessed his feelings for me. I hadn't shared that with them, of course. Linda and Sharon and I were close, but Paul was my best friend. And though they were both sort of friends with Paul, it wasn't like they really hung out or anything.

Both girls had been surprised about my crush. They thought Frank was very cute, but they echoed Paul's feelings about him: that Frank thought he was above everyone else. They both still were rooting for me, though.

But I was exactly in the same spot I'd been in back in September. These past four months, I'd never let on to Frank that I liked him. I couldn't! He'd never given me a single sign that he was interested.

Keeping my crush to myself hadn't been hard. I'd turned my energy into working like crazy for the paper, which paid off: a promotion to assistant editor in November. And that was the greatest thing, because Frank had been promoted to be one of the commentary editors in December. If I'd still been an editorial assistant, I'd have been so far out of his league that I'd have had to forget about even fantasizing about him.

So these last months I'd stared at Frank when I knew he wasn't looking. Kept my expression from turning dreamy when he talked about ideas for articles. And never once giggled, swooned, mooned, whooped, or clapped. I was a *professional,* after all. And if there was one thing *everyone* could agree on about Frank London, it was that *he* was a professional first and foremost.

At least I'd talked to him some, about writing and journalism. *I* didn't think he was a snot at all. I only thought he was amazing. He was so good at his job that even the juniors (like the other commentary editor and the two design/production staffers) and senior (sportswriter) on the staff didn't seem to mind taking direction from a sophomore. And the four other editors were sophomores. Frank's being a sophomore never posed a problem.

"So what do you think Mr. Serson's news is anyway?" I asked Linda.

She shrugged. "I'm sure it won't be anything important." Linda worked on the newspaper to keep her parents satisfied that she was participating in enough extracurricular activities. She was a features assistant, and did mostly fluff pieces. Writing wasn't the meaning of her life, the way it was for me.

"So did I tell you my latest?" Linda asked, bending over to grab a nail file out of her bag. "Dave told me Carla called him last night. She wants him back. Can you believe?"

I smiled. Linda's dating life was a constant soap opera, unlike mine, which was totally nonexistent. Other guys just didn't interest me. "At least he *told* you she called," I offered. "Most boyfriends probably wouldn't mention an ex-girlfriend calling."

"I guess." She filed her thumbnail. "Don't even

get me started on that girl, though." I half listened as she launched into a monologue about why Dave had been temporarily insane to date Carla in the first place.

The office door opened, and there he was. *He's so gorgeous,* I thought, darting glances at Frank as he sat down at a table up front. The familiar *beat-beat-beat, ping-ping-ping* of my heart was ringing so loudly in my chest, I was sure everyone could hear it.

I stared at the back of his blond head. He opened his knapsack and pulled out a stack of papers, then rifled through them. That was Frank. Always working, always serious about the paper. *He* wasn't gossiping over someone's ex. *He* wasn't wearing a stupid sweatshirt. *He* was totally confident all the time.

"Hi, all." Mr. Serson walked in and stood in front of the table that Frank was sitting behind. "Articles are due to the section editors tomorrow, as you know, but that's not the reason I called this unexpected meeting."

Linda leaned in toward me. "He is way too cute for a teacher," she whispered. "We are *so* lucky he's our advisor."

I nudged her with my elbow, and she let out a giggle.

"Neil Daldin is moving," Mr. Serson continued, "so there's an opening for the position of commentary editor."

Please don't let him announce he's chosen a girl for the job, I prayed. *That was all I needed. Some girl getting the position and working that*

closely with Frank. Let it be Jerry or Marco or—
Me.

Yeah, right. I knew Mr. Serson liked my work, but because of my crush on Frank, I had a tendency to be sort of quiet. Sometimes I was even too unsure to suggest pieces, in case Frank thought they were stupid or something. I knew that was wrong—I had really good ideas—but I couldn't help it. I spoke up half the time, which was better than nothing, wasn't it?

"Frank and I have chosen a staffer who works very long hours, writes excellent pieces, and has demonstrated an extraordinary commitment to the paper. The position is yours if you want it, Erica."

Mr. Serson was staring right at me. Frank was looking at me too.

I closed my mouth, which had dropped open. All I could do was nod, since I was totally speechless. Me! Commentary editor along with Frank London, guy of my every dream!

How incredible was this?

I took a quick look at Frank; he was smiling at me, those amazing green eyes friendly and warm. He'd never directed a smile like that at me before!

Suddenly I was acutely aware of my messy ponytail and the fact that I didn't have an ounce of makeup on my face. *Note to self,* I thought: *No more drab days. Ever.*

Linda squeezed my arm. "Congrats!" she whispered. I knew she didn't have my journalism career in mind.

I managed a smile back at Frank, then found my voice and turned my gaze to Mr. Serson. "I want it!" I announced.

God, Erica, could you try any harder to act like you're ten years old?

"Great," the teacher said. Frank nodded at me, then turned back around, his head tilted up toward Mr. Serson. "Okay, guys, that's all I really needed to tell you, so since we're all here, let's break off into sections and talk about next week's issue."

"He's yours!" Linda whispered, yanking my ponytail. The whole staff congratulated me; everyone even told me it was no surprise Serson and Frank picked me. Wow!

This was it. My chance for the job I'd dreamed of for a year and a half. And my chance to make Frank London finally notice me. Being one of the commentary editors meant I was his peer, on his level. I wasn't out of his league anymore!

I barely noticed Linda leaving her seat to meet with her group. But I was all too aware that Frank was walking toward me. Sitting down in Linda's seat. About to say something to me.

Beat-beat-beat. Ping-ping-ping.

"Congratulations." Frank extended his hand, and I slowly put mine into his. The firm contact sent tingles racing up my spine. "You're the only person we even considered for the position," he whispered.

21

Say something normal. Don't show him how nervous you are. Don't—

"Oh, me too," I blurted out.

Did that actually just come out of my mouth?

"I mean, I really wanted this position," I rushed to add. "I love working on the paper and I have so many ideas and I can't wait to dig in and get serious and—"

Frank laughed. "It's *cute* how eager you are."

He called me cute!

"Since we don't have a lot of time now," he said, "how about if we meet here tomorrow after school and go over everything? I can hear your ideas then."

"You mean just us?" I asked, cringing at the squeak in my voice.

Frank nodded. "I'm psyched to start working with you. Your pieces have been really good lately."

Psyched to start working with me! My pieces . . .
"Thanks. I mean, coming from you, that's a major compliment." I smiled at him, and he looked at me weirdly, as if he was waiting for me to say something else.

Oh!

"Right, so, tomorrow. Um, here after school. Okay!"

I can handle that just fine! I thought. At least I hoped I could. Apparently I couldn't even handle a simple conversation with the guy!

"Great," he said, standing up. "I need to show Doug a few things, so I'll see you tomorrow."

Doug? How cool was it that Frank was on a

first-name basis with Mr. Serson? He was so mature!

"Yeah, sure. I have to, um, finish up some details on an article I'm doing with Jerry." I smiled as Frank walked away, wondering if the whole room could hear my heart hammering.

I'm a commentary editor. I pressed my lips together, enjoying the sound of those words in my head. *And I'll be alone in a room with Frank London tomorrow!*

Where was Paul? I glanced at the doorway to my history classroom for the fiftieth time in the past thirty seconds. Still no sign of him.

I grabbed my knapsack off the back of my seat and pulled out my red notebook. I used red for this class because red made me think of war, which was pretty much the major thing you learned about in history. Paul was the only one who knew about my dorky habit of color-coding my notebooks, and he'd given up teasing me about it years ago.

Leaning back in my scat, I took a deep breath and reviewed how to present my news to him. He'd be thrilled for me about the position. But as for working with Frank . . . *that* could get sticky.

It had been tough getting our friendship back on track since he'd told me about his feelings for me. He'd avoided me for a couple of weeks, and I didn't push it, knowing he'd need the time away from me. When he'd finally appeared at my doorstep one day with two tickets to the hottest horror flick, I knew things would be okay. And they had been. He'd never asked me about Frank, and since there was never anything to tell, I'd never brought it up. He acted totally normal around me, the way he always had.

After a month, it was as though the whole conversation had never even happened. Sometimes I'd think about it, and I figured he did too. But we never, ever talked about it again. There were occasional moments of awkwardness, like if Linda or Sharon mentioned Frank in Paul's presence. But he never said anything. I had a feeling he'd be happy for me if Frank and I hooked up. Maybe jealous or even upset, but happy for me nonetheless. He was my best friend.

"Hey, Park! Wake up!"

I jerked my head up; Paul was sliding into the seat next to me. He looked totally psyched about something. I decided that I shouldn't mention the *Postscript* thing. Just in case.

"I ran into Linda and she told me you got the commentary job," he said. "That's awesome!"

Was that why he seemed so psyched? Because he'd heard the news and knew how much it meant to me? Even though Linda had probably mentioned something about Frank? Paul *was* that good a friend.

"I couldn't believe it!" I exclaimed. "You should have seen me—I couldn't even talk. Me, Erica Park, commentary editor! And then—" I cut myself off, unsure if I should mention the Frank thing. Maybe Linda *hadn't* brought it up?

"And then what?" Paul prodded.

I bit my lip. "And then everyone else said really

nice stuff too. You know, like how much I deserve this and everything."

"You totally do," he replied. "So, I guess you'll be working really closely with Frank London."

I swallowed, then nodded, watching his expression. Nothing. He clearly wasn't congratulating me the way Linda had, but he didn't look upset either.

"I know that must make you happy, Park," he said, "so start smiling. It's okay. Really."

I reached over to hug him.

"Why don't you two just get married already!" Vanessa Peid joked from behind us.

We broke apart and gave each other little grins. "I've got great news too," Paul said. He had that shy look on his face, the one where his mouth crinkled at the corners and his eyes almost looked closed.

"I asked out Katie Wing," he whispered. "And she said yes."

"Wow!" I exclaimed, surprised. Katie was Paul's chemistry partner. He'd been saying nice stuff about her for a while, but it had never even crossed my mind that he was into her. "I can't believe you didn't tell me you liked her!"

"I didn't want to jinx it by saying anything," he replied. "It's no big deal, though. Just a date. See how it goes, you know."

"This *is* a big deal!" I exclaimed. "I mean, you're finally—you've, um . . ." I knew my cheeks must be bright red. I looked at Paul uncertainly.

"It's okay," he told me, smiling. "I really like

her. And I think she kind of likes me too. I mean, I *hope* so."

"I don't think I can bear another minute of your huge ego," I teased, hoping to lighten the mood. "You've *got* to turn it down a notch."

Paul laughed.

Our teacher entered the classroom, so Paul and I turned our attention toward what he was writing on the blackboard. *Wow,* I thought. Paul was actually interested in another girl. This was the first time in nearly a year that he'd asked out anyone. I darted a glance at him; he had a totally blissful look on his face.

So this was really great, right? Paul would date Katie, they'd fall madly in love, and maybe Frank would finally notice me and we'd become this major couple. Both Paul and I would be really happy, and we'd definitely still be the same best friends. Maybe we could even double-date.

Katie Wing, huh? She didn't exactly seem to be Paul's type—kind of flighty, and very girlie. But so what? *I'm sure she's nice if Paul likes her,* I thought happily. *And I'm glad he's moving on.* That was definitely a good thing. I *wanted* him to like someone else, didn't I? And now that he did, there was nothing holding me—or my heart—back.

Two

"ERICA PARK, REPORTING for duty," I announced as I walked into the *Postscript* office. *Reporting for duty? Well, at least it only took me two seconds to reveal what a geek I am.*

But Frank barely seemed to hear me. He was hunched over the computer, deeply involved in something. "Uh . . . uh-huh," he said distractedly.

I sat down. Today I was wearing a miniskirt, which was rare for me (I'd borrowed it from Sharon), black tights, and the cool black shoes that hurt my feet. I had on my lucky sweater, a fuzzy periwinkle-colored thing that Paul had bought me for Christmas two years ago. A major improvement from yesterday. My hair was down and brushed and shiny. And I had on just enough makeup to look somewhat okay, but not as though I was *trying*. Both Linda and Sharon had coached me on that after school.

I stared at the back of his head as he pecked away

at the keyboard. And stared. And stared. After a full five minutes I started fidgeting, but then he finally turned around. "Sorry about that," he said, gesturing at the computer behind him. "I was in the middle of a very complex thought."

"Oh, I totally understand," I reassured him. "I know how hard it is to stop when you're caught up in an idea."

He nodded. "Neil used to flip out when I wouldn't give him my full attention right away." He sighed. "You'd think a *junior* would be mature enough to let someone concentrate. No loss seeing him go."

So he was implying that I was mature, since I didn't whine about being ignored and made to wait. That was good. The last thing I wanted him to know was just how little patience I had. That was something that Paul loved about me—he had all the patience in the world.

I was surprised to hear Frank talk negatively about Neil, though; everyone thought Neil was totally cool and was disappointed he was leaving Emerson.

"Let me clear some room for you," Frank said, standing up and collecting his pile of papers in a stack. *Could his shoulders be any broader?* I wondered, once again staring at his back. *He is so hot!*

He grabbed a piece of paper and glanced down at it. "This is so stupid," he said. "I can't even believe this is what Serson thinks is newsworthy." He handed me the paper and I skimmed it quickly.

It was Linda's piece on what girls wanted as gifts from their boyfriends or crushes for Valentine's Day, which was in two weeks. The whole idea struck me as kind of silly too. I wouldn't say it was *stupid,* though. Just sort of sappy. Almost like a PDA in print or something.

"I guess it is pretty pathetic," I agreed, handing back the article. "I mean the *subject,*" I rushed to add, "not Linda's writing, which is really good, though it could use some editing." I cringed. I couldn't believe I'd put down my own friend in front of Frank! He had a lot of pull with Mr. Serson. What if he thought Linda should be off the paper?

"That's the mark of a true professional," Frank said, tossing the piece back into the in box. "I've noticed that you and Linda are good friends, so I'm impressed that you're professional enough to evaluate her work objectively." He grinned at me. "I wouldn't say her writing is *really* good, though. It's *okay.* Doesn't touch yours with a ten-foot pole."

I felt myself beam at the compliment. Frank just wasn't into fluff pieces, that was all. It made sense that he wouldn't be into anything Linda wrote.

"I told Doug I didn't want us doing a big issue on Valentine's Day," Frank said. I had to remind myself that he meant Mr. Serson. "But he overruled me, insisting that people love it. Newspapers really shouldn't have such sentimental stuff. It's so corny and stupid."

"I know what you mean," I said. "It drives me crazy when I work forever on a serious article, like

29

that one I did on the need for student volunteers at the hospital—"

"That was an excellent piece, by the way," Frank interrupted, and my heart rate zoomed. He definitely respected me.

"Thanks," I replied. "Anyway, that ended up coming out in the same issue as the review of the back-to-school dance, and the dance was all anyone read or talked about."

Frank smiled sympathetically. "Get used to it. The Valentine's Day special edition will disappear much faster than the paper usually does. It's just the mentality here."

Wow. He actually used words like *mentality*— words that my friends always teased me for saying. SAT words, they called them.

"It's so funny that everyone gets all worked up over Valentine's Day," I mused, leaning back in my chair. "It's such a *ridiculous* holiday. It's like a free-for-all for PDA."

"I completely agree!" Frank exclaimed. "I thought I was the only one left who didn't buy into that stuff."

So did I, I thought, twitching with excitement.

We *were* meant for each other!

"Hey, so what if we do an *anti*–Valentine's Day article for that issue?" I suggested.

Frank tilted his head. "What do you have in mind?"

"Well, the features articles will probably be sappy and silly, right?"

"Got that right." He gestured toward the in box.

I bit back a grin. "So we can write an objective commentary on how silly the whole thing is, how people expect all this stuff just because it's February fourteenth, when it doesn't really mean anything. Like last year, three couples I know broke up because the guys blew it with presents. One girl threw a fit because her boyfriend didn't buy her a candygram. Can you believe that? A *two-dollar* bag of candy you order from the school store and that gets delivered in front of everyone on Valentine's Day. Big deal! It's all so ridiculous! The expectations, the hurt, the obligations—"

"I love it!" Frank responded. "We'll analyze the holiday in a totally unsentimental way to show everyone how stupid they act. Erica, you're brilliant!"

Brilliant. I love it . . .

"Sort of a sociological and psychological study on human reaction." Frank's amazing green eyes sparkled. "It'll be the thinking man's article on Valentine's Day."

You're the one who's brilliant, I thought. Frank was the only person I knew who could talk like that.

"This is great." He grabbed a yellow legal pad from the desk and started scribbling notes. "You've got to work on this one yourself. I don't trust any of our other writers with it. I mean, you and I are probably the only ones who'll even *get* it. But once everyone reads it . . . we'll totally reshape public opinion!"

A thrill of pride rushed through me. *Reshape*

public opinion. How cool was that? Even *Paul* would see that PDAs were gross once we explained it in a way that really made people stop and think.

"Let's turn the whole commentary section into an anti-Valentine's section. We'll take the holiday *so* seriously that people will see how crazy it is to take it seriously."

"That's perfect!" I exclaimed. "I can interview everyone on their opinions and expectations, but show it from a different perspective than Linda did in her piece. I know she won't mind. Plus it's so amazing that we'll present both sides in the paper. That's the way it *should* be."

Frank nodded. "Hey, while you're working on it from that angle, I can write a serious piece about the history of the holiday. No one ever talks about that." He dropped the pen and pad down on the desk. "Thank God Neil is outta here! Working with you is going to be . . ." His voice trailed off as he glanced down for a second, then back up at me. "Really, really great," he finished.

Beat-beat-beat, ping-ping-ping.

I realized I was staring at his lips, wondering what it would be like to kiss him.

He handed me a pad, then turned back around and hunched over the desk, scribbling like mad. I was so inspired! I started scribbling too—my ideas came so fast: whom to interview, what questions to ask, who the class couples were, what the stores had in the windows to attract people who were in the market for candy and stuffed animals and jewelry.

"Wow," he said, turning around. "It's getting really late. I've gotta get home."

"Oh, me too," I replied, glancing at my watch, though I could have stayed there for hours and hours and hours more.

"So I guess we'll talk soon about how we'll divide up the commentary section?" I said as I packed up my bag. "I mean, in general, not just for the Valentine's issue. And we should probably meet in addition to the staff meetings, right?" *Do I sound as pathetically desperate to spend more time with this guy as I think I do?*

"Yeah, definitely," Frank agreed. "Friday night?"

I blinked. *Is he asking me out?*

"Um, sure," I said.

"Maybe over dinner?" he continued.

Dinner on a Friday night has to be a date, I reassured myself.

"Okay." That was definitely not an SAT-word kind of response.

"Cool," he said. "I'll see you tomorrow night, then. We can talk more about how we're going to structure the Valentine's Day commentary section."

I nodded. "See you tomorrow." I grabbed my backpack and strolled out, resisting the urge to skip down the hallway. *That* would not be mature.

"Hi, everybody, I'm home!" I yelled. I dropped my backpack in the hall and ran into the kitchen.

I stopped dead in my tracks. Paul was sitting at the long oak table with my little brother, Charlie.

My dad stood over the stove, stirring something that smelled delicious. "Hi, honey," Dad said over his shoulder. "Your mom and Ellen went to the store to pick up soda. Oh, and Paul's here."

"Really?" I kidded. *Shouldn't Paul be obsessing over what to wear on his date with Katie or something?* "What's up?" I asked him. "Here for my dad's amazing beef stew?" Paul had eaten at my house so many times over the years that my parents joked he was using me for their cooking.

All I wanted to do was float up to my room and think about the following night. Frank and me on a date. At dinner. Sitting across from each other. I wanted to go over all the wonderful things he'd said to me that day. And I couldn't exactly dream away with Paul here.

"He's here to see *me*," Charlie announced proudly. "Right, Paul?"

"Of course, kiddo." Paul winked at me. "But now that your sister's home I should probably hang out with her a little so she doesn't get too jealous.

"So where were you?" Paul asked as we headed into the living room, plopping down on the overstuffed sofa. "I came by over an hour ago, sure you'd be here by then. Charlie and I made it to the fifth board in that new PlayStation game."

"Newspaper stuff," I said. "Why'd you stop by?"

Paul grinned, then got up and grabbed his backpack. "Close your eyes," he instructed, sitting back down.

"What's going on?" I asked.

"Just do it, silly."

I shut my eyes.

"Okay, here." He placed something that felt like a book in my hands. "Now open them."

In my hands was a collection of Anna Quindlen's columns from her days at the *New York Times*. Paul knew she was my idol.

"Thank you," I said, my heart squeezing in my chest. This was so incredibly thoughtful. "I love it! But what's the occasion?"

Paul rolled his eyes. "Read the message, dope."

I opened the book; a note in Paul's messy handwriting was scribbled on the first page.

To my best friend,

Congratulations on your new gig at the *Postscript*. I am so proud of you, and I'm sure that someday you'll be autographing your own book of columns. I'll always be your biggest fan, no matter what.

Love, Paul

No matter what. I put the book down and looked up at Paul, who was smiling shyly. "This is so perfect," I said, throwing my arms around him. "Thank you so much."

He pulled back after giving me a quick squeeze. "You're welcome. And congratulations again, kid."

"Hey, so, how's everything going with Katie?" I asked.

"Great. She seems really excited about our date," Paul said. It killed me how clueless he was as to how much girls liked him.

"And are you excited too?" I asked, curious.

He blushed a little. "I think . . . I think she's pretty amazing. She had on these killer jeans today, with this little pink shirt—"

"Good. That's good . . . great!" I said brightly, cutting him off. Katie Wing's wardrobe did not interest me. "And I, um, actually have a date this weekend too."

"Oh, yeah?" Paul said, his eyes widening with mock surprise. "Who's the unlucky guy?"

"Frank London." I fingered a tassel of the mohair throw on the arm of the sofa. "He asked me out." I grinned. "Finally."

Paul frowned. "Finally? I thought you'd be over him by now. Now that you've gotten to know him, that is."

"What's that supposed to mean?" I said, irritated. I didn't expect Paul to throw me a party or anything, but I at least thought he'd be happy for me. He knew how much I liked Frank, and how long I'd waited for this to happen.

Paul just shrugged. "I guess I thought once you got to know him a little, you'd be turned off. You should see him at our yearbook meetings. He acts like he's the king of everything."

I crossed my arms. "I don't know what you're talking about. He's always been nice to me."

"He didn't even know who you were until a few days ago," Paul said thickly.

"Well, he knows me now," I retorted. "At our meeting today we clicked on everything. Like this

36

anti-Valentine's Day article I suggested. He wants to do a whole *section* now."

"Now that's impressive," Paul muttered. "Who knew anyone else hated hearts and flowers as much as you do?"

"Exactly," I said. "So can you maybe try to be a little happy for me?"

Paul flashed a fake smile. "There. I'm happy."

I nudged his foot. "Come on. I'm finally going out with the guy I've had a crush on all year. I'm sorry you don't like him, but I do. And I'm the one who's going out with him." My heart pitter-patted at the words. I was going out with Frank London! I couldn't wait to tell Linda and Sharon. I smiled at Paul. "Hey, you don't have time to stress me out over this anyway. You've got to start planning your date with Katie."

"Yeah." He stretched his legs out. "I want to find somewhere really—"

"Erica!" My dad's voice boomed from the kitchen. "Dinner's ready."

I glanced at Paul. "Are you gonna stay?"

He shook his head, jumping up. "I should get home."

I grabbed his hand and squeezed. "Thanks again for the book. I love it."

"I'm glad. Tell your folks I said bye. And tell Charlie I'll be back for a rematch soon."

"Okay. And if you need help planning your date or anything, I'd be glad to help," I offered.

"You, the anti-romantic? I'd be better off having

Bill and Steve from the basketball team come to my rescue." He grinned. "Nah, I can handle it myself, Erica. But thanks, though."

"Sure," I said, walking him to the door and watching him jog away. I wondered where he would take Katie? To a fancy restaurant? A movie? The mall?

Then a better thought hit me. Where would Frank be taking *me*?

Three

*I*CAN'T BELIEVE *I'm in a real restaurant on a real date with Frank London!* I thought for the third time as I watched him study his menu. Thank God I hadn't worn jeans. After almost two hours of raiding my closet (and three calls each to Sharon and Linda), I'd finally settled on the black pants and the ice-blue sweater I'd gotten at the mall a couple of weeks earlier. I'd been planning on jeans and a nice sweater, but Linda had said no way, and Sharon seconded her. Frank was sophisticated, they insisted. And that meant a real outfit.

I'm so grateful I have friends who know these things, I thought as I looked around the elegant Italian restaurant. We were sitting in a candlelit booth with cloth napkins and water goblets. The name of the place was La Dolce Vita. Frank had told me that meant "the sweet life," and it certainly felt like it to me. Beautiful artwork decorated the walls, and the only light came from a slender candle in the center of our table.

"This place is amazing," I whispered. It seemed wrong to talk too loudly there. "It was really great of your dad to drive us."

He glanced up at me and smiled, and something inside my chest went flippety-flop. *So that's what it means when people talk about their hearts going flip-flop.*

"I knew you'd like it," he said, his gorgeous eyes impossibly greener. Was it due to the romantic lighting? The dark green turtleneck he looked so incredible in? "Do you know what you want to eat?"

Thank God for that subdued lighting, I thought in terror as I glanced back down at my own menu. My flushed cheeks would give away that I didn't recognize a single thing on the page. I'd never even heard of any of the pastas. "Um, I'm not sure yet."

"Their penne vodka is fabulous," he told me.

Penne what? My knowledge of Italian food didn't extend beyond spaghetti and meatballs. No way was I confessing to that.

"Sounds good," I replied in a confident tone. "Is that what you're having?"

Frank nodded. "It's my favorite dish."

"May I take your order?" A waiter suddenly hovered over us.

I gulped. I had this silly shyness problem with waiters, salespeople, cashiers—they totally intimidated me. My first year at sleep-away camp, I'd eaten nothing but salad bar stuff for the first week because I couldn't handle the idea of announcing what I wanted on the hot-food line. I'd improved a lot over the years, but situations like this were still nerve-wracking. Whenever Paul and I went anywhere, he always did the ordering for me, and he never teased me about it.

But Paul wasn't there. And I couldn't exactly tell Frank London I was incapable of telling a waiter what I wanted for dinner.

"I'll have the penne vodka," Frank told the waiter, handing him his menu.

"Very good." The waiter made a little note on his order pad, then turned to me. I felt the familiar heat rise to my face. "And the lady?"

"Excuse me?" I asked the waiter, darting an embarrassed glance at Frank.

"What will you be having?" the waiter rephrased.

"I'll have the same," I blurted out, relieved when he left.

"My family doesn't eat out a lot, really," I said, feeling like I needed to explain my clumsiness. No one I knew ate out for dinner, unless it was for some celebration. La Dolce Vita was the kind of restaurant my parents went to for their anniversary.

Frank took a sip of his ice water, which had a lemon wedge on the edge of the glass.

"So, how's that article on the Maryland water system going?" I asked, eager to distract him from thinking about how unworldly I was in comparison to him. I knew Frank had been working on the

41

piece for a couple of weeks, in addition to his regular duties at the *Postscript.*

Frank's face lit up. "Doug took a look at what I have so far, and he said I should send it to the *Baltimore Sun.*"

"Are you *serious?*" I asked. "Wow."

He nodded. "Doug says it's one of the best commentary pieces he's seen at our school, ever." He frowned. "Of course, it seems pretty pointless to bother publishing it in the *Postscript.*"

Okay, the *Postscript* wasn't the *Sun,* but he didn't really think our paper was worthless, did he?

"Your stuff is wonderful," Frank said, as though he'd read my mind. He reached across the table to take my hand. "For a high school paper it's not that bad, but . . "

I froze for a second, so aware of the feel of his fingers, warm and strong and male, caressing my own. This had to mean he was attracted to me, right? Even when he slid his hand back, I could still feel the imprint.

"You're the only one on staff who can write," he continued.

He really thinks highly of me, I realized. All these months I'd been so nervous about his opinion of me, and he'd respected my work all along. But I wasn't the only staffer who could string a sentence together. Everyone on the staff could write really well.

"So have you decided how to approach the Valentine's article research?" Frank asked.

I nodded. "I'm going to base it on interviews

and observation around the halls. I'll do something on couples' behavior in general, which can be beyond ridiculous, and then how couples are affected by Valentine's Day."

"Sounds great," Frank said. "I can't wait to see what you come up with."

The waiter placed two steaming bowls of short, tubelike pasta in a rich, thick pinkish sauce in front of us. The pasta looked delicious—and smelled amazing.

But I could barely eat. My appetite was wiped out by this bizarre happy-excited–nervous thing that had taken over my stomach. This was so weird! All these feelings. What the simple touch of his hand on mine could do. How one little smile of his turned my knees all wobbly.

This is the definition of sappy, sentimental, goo, I thought, and suddenly understood what Paul had meant when he'd told me, "If you felt that way about someone, you wouldn't find PDAs so gross."

But Paul was still way wrong about that. One little hand squeeze was not a PDA. It was a tasteful gesture to indicate romantic feeling.

I forced myself to swallow some forkfuls of the pasta. It *was* really delicious.

Even after we both finished, neither of us mentioned how late it had gotten or that we should head home. We'd talked about writing and journalism for most of the meal—we had so much in common. I could never talk to Paul or Sharon or even Linda about the nitty-gritty of journalism, basically because I didn't want to bore them to tears. But with Frank, I could talk about it forever.

The waiter placed a leather billfold of sorts on the table, and Frank looked inside, then took his wallet out of his back pocket and slid out a credit card, which he put inside the billfold. He had a credit card? Talk about sophisticated! No one I knew had one.

"Dinner's on me, of course," he said, smiling that incredible smile. "And it's my pleasure."

"Thank you, Frank," I whispered. We looked directly into each other's eyes for a moment without saying anything. He was so mature. So grown-up. So leaps and bounds above the average sophomore. And he definitely liked me!

"Erica, I have a proposal for you," he said.

A proposal?

"Well, you know how the Valentine's Day issue of the *Postscript* isn't coming out till the Tuesday *after* Valentine's?" he began.

"Yeah," I said, praying that he couldn't tell I was holding my breath. "That way the features crew can write about the dance Saturday night and print the pictures."

"So I thought maybe *we* should go to the dance together," Frank said. "We can take notes for a special article on the dance itself. The anti-dance article. What a scream that'll be!"

Flip-flop. Flip-flop.

I was so stunned I couldn't even speak. The guy of my dreams was asking me to the Valentine's dance—and weeks in advance!

"For research purposes, of course," Frank added.

Research purposes? That was *too* adorable—Frank actually thought he needed an *excuse* to ask me to the dance. I had never thought Frank London could be anything but totally confident. But now he was showing a side of himself I hadn't seen. A vulnerable side. A not-so-secure side. And it was me who was making him unsure!

"That's a great idea, Frank."

He smiled that incredible smile and squeezed my hand.

Frank London was practically my boyfriend!

The second I shut my bedroom door I flopped down on my bed, actual giggles coming out of my mouth, which had been in huge-smile mode ever since Frank's dad dropped me off after our date.

Giggles. The same ridiculous sounds Linda made when Mr. Serson complimented her. The sound that had always made me want to gag.

I'd been on dates. I'd even been on dates with guys who had half a clue. But in my whole romantic history, I'd never come home feeling like this before.

Was this what being in love felt like?

The phone meowed, and I snatched up Garfield's head. The cartoon-cat telephone was a gift from Paul, of course, who knew I loved stuff like that. Every birthday and holiday he got me one real present and a joke item, something as outrageous as possible. My room was full of fun presents from Paul.

"Hello?" I said.

"Home from your dream date already? Surprise, surprise."

I tried to ignore Paul's sarcasm. "If you didn't think I would be, why'd you call?"

Paul paused. "I figured Frank would do something so obnoxious you'd run away from him screaming. I was just checking up on you."

"Paul . . ."

"Just kidding," he interrupted, and I could hear the mischievous smile in his voice. "So, you had a good time?"

"An *incredible* time," I gushed. "The restaurant was amazing! And he asked me to the Valentine's dance! Isn't that cool?"

"Wait a minute," Paul said. "The two biggest anti-sap cynics are actually going to a school dance? And on the day of looove, no less?"

"Well, Frank and I are way above looking at it like *that*," I explained. "We'll be working too—we're gonna do research for the article we're writing on the dance, how dumb all the hoopla is. Isn't it *so* me and *so* him that he asked in such a clever *us* way?"

Silence. "So it's like a work thing?" he asked after a few more seconds of dead air. "Not like you're going to the dance *together?*"

"Of course we're going *together*," I said. "I mean, we'll dance, drink punch, the whole works. But given how we both feel about all that stuff, it made perfect sense for him to act like he was asking for *Postscript* reasons."

"But if you both feel that way about the dance, why would you even go in the first place? I mean, if you're both so above it? Unless it really is about writing the anti-sap, anti-dance, anti-Valentine's article."

Silence. Was he trying to make me mad? "Well, of course it's about that. That's our whole point, Paul. But we're *allowed* to like each other too. Give me a break, okay? So," I said, dying to get off the subject of me and Frank, "are you going to ask Katie to the dance?"

"If everything goes as great as I think it will tomorrow night, then yep, I'm gonna ask her. Romantically, though. I hope that doesn't make you too sick."

I laughed. Paul totally understood me. Okay, he didn't like Frank. At all. But he understood me, he respected me, just like I respected him. We simply had different ideas about romance, that was all. Paul was all about putting his feelings out there, being ooey-gooey. Kissing and holding hands. Sweet stuff. The kind of stuff I was feeling *inside* about Frank.

I'd always thought that when I met the guy of my dreams, he'd be just like Paul, but I'd feel those *feelings*. Those feelings I'd never had for Paul because he was like my brother, my best friend in the world since we were five. So now I had those feelings, but the guy was *nothing* like Paul at all.

That was sort of weird.

I couldn't imagine Frank giving me a Garfield phone for Christmas. Insisting on a french-fry-eating contest. Racing me down the block backward. That was Paul. But I could imagine Frank giving me that book, the collection of essays by my favorite journalist. Yet that was Paul too.

"Oh!" Paul said suddenly. "I almost forgot to tell you . . . hold on a sec." I heard papers being thrown around, and pictured Paul rummaging through his less-than-tidy room. "Found it," he said. "Don't miss the annual Comic Book Lover's convention," he read aloud. "February fourteenth at the Baltimore convention center from one to four."

"Oh, cool!" I exclaimed. "I was wondering when that would be this year." The comic book convention was one of our many traditions, probably my favorite. Paul and I went every year and spent hours walking through the aisles of endless comics, wishing we could buy every single one. And a lot of people came dressed up as their favorite superheroes. It was so much fun!

I grabbed my calendar and wrote *Comic book c.* in the box for February fourteenth.

"Are you sure you still want to go, though?" he asked.

"Huh?" I said, writing *V-day dance with Frank* below the comic book notation. I drew a little heart around Frank's name. "Why wouldn't I?"

"Hel-lo? It's on Valentine's Day. You still wanna go?"

"Of course." I paused, not sure what he was getting at. "Again, Garabo—why wouldn't I? It's in the afternoon, so we'll both still have plenty of time to get ready for the dance."

"Great, so we'll go," he said.

I leaned back and rested my head on my pillow, my calendar on my stomach. "I should probably get to sleep," I said.

"Me too," Paul agreed. "I'll give you a call tomorrow before I pick up Katie, so you can help ease my panic attack."

"Good night," I said.

"Sweet dreams," he told me, and hung up.

Sweet dreams. Exactly what I expected to have.

I picked up my calendar and stared at the notations for the fourteenth. *V-day dance with Frank.* Another giggle came out of my mouth.

And then I bolted upright.

I'd drawn a heart around Frank's name. When had I done that? It was exactly the kind of thing I was supposed to be *against*. Exactly the kind of thing I planned to poke fun at in my anti-sap, anti–Valentine's article.

Weird. Very weird.

Erica: Do you have any special Valentine's Day memories?

Linda: My favorite one was with my first boyfriend, Randy Thomas. It was either sixth or seventh grade. I'm pretty sure it was sixth, because I had shorter hair then. Unless maybe it was—

Erica: What made the day so great?

Linda: I guess because I finally had a guy do all that stuff for me. You know, the candy, the flowers and everything. It was sixth grade, definitely.

Erica: So it wasn't that you really *liked* Randy that much. You just wanted the *stuff.* Okay, next question. What do you see as the purpose of the holiday?

Linda: Oh, wait, can we go back to the last question? I *liked* him. Really liked him. I was so upset when he dumped me—I cried for, like, an entire weekend. Anyway, what did you ask? Oh, right. I think the purpose is that it's one day where you show how much you like each other. You know how guys can be—they don't talk about their feelings or do nice things that often. So on Valentine's Day, they're, like, *supposed* to or maybe *allowed* to. If they give you a mushy card and a really great present and take you out to dinner, their friends won't rank on them, because they're supposed to be doing that on Valentine's Day.

Erica: So are you saying it's okay for guys to act like jerks all year and then it's all made up for on Valentine's Day? Just because a guy gives you a box of chocolates? That seems sort of weird, you know?

Linda: Guys are guys. That's just the way it is. Why do you think girls make such a big deal of Valentine's Day? Because they can finally expect a little mush from their boyfriends. Makes total sense to me.

Four

"I WONDER HOW she'll choose to bore us today," Frank whispered in my ear as Principal Martin ambled onto the auditorium stage for our weekly Monday morning assembly.

I chuckled. "Maybe it'll be the keep-the-school-clean speech." Mrs. Martin, a round little woman with a huge pouf of orange-red hair, was definitely a little dull.

Then again, the way things were going, I'd think anything was possible—even an interesting address from our principal. After all, who would have expected Frank to wait outside my homeroom so that we could sit together at the assembly?

That was definitely romantic.

"Good morning, students of Emerson High," Mrs. Martin began. "I was thinking this weekend about responsibility. . . ."

"Nope," I murmured to Frank. "It's the one about homework."

He grinned at me. I loved that we were able to joke around—maybe there was a little Paul in him, after all.

As Mrs. Martin rambled on about the importance of studying, I realized I had the perfect opportunity to study couples in the audience—see how close they sat to each other, whether or not they held hands, if they were staring at each other or actually paying attention to the principal.

Anthony Perez and Shay-Lee Ibanez. They were seniors and a *major* item at Emerson High. I studied the way they leaned into each other, how he held her hand in his lap. How she even stretched her free left hand all the way around to scratch an itch on her right shoulder. Was that sappy? Or was it sweet?

I'd been so busy looking at couples that I barely registered Mrs. Martin calling up the yearbook advisor, Mr. Kensington, onto the stage for a special announcement.

Mr. Kensington announced that the election for school historian would be held in two weeks, and that those running could officially put up campaign posters starting the next day. He mentioned something about a debate, where students could hear what the candidates had planned. The school historian was responsible for documenting the highs and lows of the year in the yearbook. It was a pretty big deal at Emerson High.

I looked around the auditorium for more couples to study as Mr. Kensington went on and on.

Whoa! Was that Paul and Katie sitting *this close* to each other? They weren't holding hands or anything, but her hair was practically brushing his shoulder!

Paul had called me before and after his date with Katie on Saturday night. And then he'd gone over every detail over our usual fries at the Bowl-a-Rama's snack bar on Sunday. He and Katie had gotten along great and kissed twice. On the lips.

Frank and I hadn't kissed on the lips on our first date. But I was willing to bet he was an amazing kisser.

I wonder what kind of kisser Paul is?

The thought jolted me to sit up straight. Where had *that* come from? Paul and I had hugged and kissed a thousand times. Not a date kiss, of course, but pecks on the lips were no big deal for us. I stole another glance at Paul and Katie. She was looking into his eyes—they were deep in conversation about something.

"Earth to Erica . . ." Frank was grinning at me. I hadn't even noticed the assembly had ended. "Did you even hear a word Kensington said?"

"Every single one," I lied as we stood up to file out. I wouldn't want him to know I'd zoned out during his yearbook advisor's speech. "Hey, so are you interested in running for historian?" We were crammed in among a gazillion students trying to leave the auditorium.

"Definitely," he said. "I really want to win."

"Won't it be a ton of work?" I asked. "You've

got so much responsibility on the paper, and you're in all the advanced classes."

"I need challenges, Erica," he said. "Otherwise I'd be totally bored."

I knew I was gazing at him—and with that awestruck look in my eyes. But I couldn't help it. He was so ambitious. So driven. So capable of anything.

"You know," he said, leaning closer to me, "sometimes these elections are nothing but popularity contests. A lot of people know who I am, but I kind of stand apart from the crowd. So, if more partying types run for historian, I could actually lose. And that would be a real shame for the whole school—I'd work my butt off, take it really seriously."

"I'd vote for you," I said, grinning.

"Hey—would you be interested in helping out with my campaign?" he asked. "You're such a great writer, and I'll bet you could come up with catchy slogans. Plus you could help me write my speech for the debate. It would be like we're a team, just like we are at the *Postscript*."

A team . . .

"Wow, so I'd be sort of like your campaign manager," I said. Could I have been any more thrilled? I actually had to keep my joy in check; otherwise I might have started jumping up and down! "Count me in."

This was so flattering. He was asking for *my* help. Frank London!

I couldn't wait to tell Paul!

★　　　★　　　★

"That's incredible!" Linda exclaimed, slamming her locker door shut.

"What's incredible?" Sharon asked as she came up on us.

"Get this," Linda said to Sharon. "First Frank takes her to some expensive restaurant *and* asks her to the Valentine's dance. Now the guy wants her help in his campaign for school historian. He's definitely in love!"

"Do you think so?" I asked eagerly. "Does all this really mean he likes me, like, a lot? Girlfriend-boyfriend territory?"

Linda stared at me, then placed her palm against my forehead. "Are you feeling okay? Coming down with a fever? Because this is definitely not the Erica Park I know. You're really gone!"

Sharon laughed and twisted her long blond hair into a knot at the back of her neck. "So maybe he's not such a snot after all. He sounds pretty cool."

"He is," I assured her. "Really, really, really cool. He's so different from other guys."

"Does Paul still hate his guts?" Sharon asked. "It can be so weird if your best guy friend thinks your boyfriend is slime."

I'd mentioned to Linda and Sharon that Frank *wasn't* Paul's favorite person. Both girls thought maybe Paul was jealous that another guy would take all my time. They had no idea how close to the truth they were. But during the rest of the weekend I'd been wondering if jealousy really had anything to do with it. He seemed to dislike Frank for reasons based on his *own* experiences with him.

"He's *not* my boyfriend—yet," I corrected Sharon. "I'm sure Paul will think he's just as cool as you guys do once he gets to know him a little."

But what if he didn't? What if my best friend and my boyfriend-to-be hated each other's guts?

I scanned the cafeteria for Paul, balancing my lunch tray carefully so the salad wouldn't end up with root beer dressing. There he was: I'd know that thick glossy hair and fuzzball navy sweater anywhere. I couldn't wait to share my news about helping Frank with his campaign. Paul thought politics were cool.

I weaved my way to one of the open seats at Paul's table. I hadn't realized that Katie was there too.

"Erica, hi," Paul said. "I'm glad you found us."

"Yeah, hi," I said, noticing how Katie's hand was loosely wrapped around Paul's arm.

"Hi, Erica," Katie said. Today her hair was in a tight braid that she'd tossed over her shoulder. Self-consciously I fingered my own shoulder-length locks. Paul had had a fit when I'd cut my hair a few years ago. It had once been longer than Katie's.

But long hair was over, I told myself.

"We were just talking about this funny thing that happened in chem. today," Paul explained. He looked at Katie, who dissolved into laughter.

I nodded, unsure what to do. Did they want to keep talking about it privately? I glanced around the cafeteria. It was too crowded to go elsewhere. Feeling like a third wheel, I put down my tray and slid into the seat across from Paul.

"So what happened?" I asked, sticking my fork in my salad. I didn't like how awkward I felt. "What was so funny?"

"Well, see, Brian Potter took out this beaker—" Paul began.

"And then Mrs. Hunt walked into the room—" Katie picked up. Then she looked at Paul and they both cracked up.

"You had to be there," Paul said, shaking his head.

I managed a small smile. "Sounds like it."

"So how's your day going?" Katie asked cheerfully, her chair awfully close to Paul's. Were they holding hands under the table? I fought back the urge to peer under the table and find out.

"It's fine," I said politely, chewing a tasteless tomato. I noted that she had a small pimple forming on her left cheek. For some reason, that made me happy.

For a minute or so, no one said anything. I couldn't believe that I was actually feeling awkward around Paul. It was like Katie's presence had wedged my vocal cords shut.

"So, Katie," I said, racking my brain for something friendly to say. I owed it to Paul to be nice to this girl, whatever she was to him.

"Erica!"

I looked up, surprised.

Frank smiled down at me, his blond hair wind-blown and incredibly sexy. He held a brown paper bag in his hand. "Hey, this seat free?" he asked, gesturing to the one beside me.

"Sure!" I said, grinning at him. Not only had he saved me from a really awkward situation, this was a perfect opportunity for Paul to get to know him. To see what I saw.

Frank nodded at Paul and Katie as he took his seat. "Have you interviewed anyone for the Valentine's section yet?" he asked before taking a huge bite of chicken salad.

"Just one person so far," I told him, wishing I'd done more interviews. I'd been so anxious about doing a good job that I'd put off even starting; Linda was my only interviewee to date.

"Hey, have you interviewed these two?" Frank gestured to Paul and Katie. "How long have you guys been a couple?"

"Not long enough," Katie said with a giggle. Paul smiled, but I could tell he was uncomfortable.

"Then you guys would be perfect!" Frank said eagerly. "It'd be great to interview couples at different stages," he told me, raising his eyebrows as if I was supposed to pick up the hint.

"I think that sounds like fun," Katie announced. "I'd love for you to interview us, Erica." She put her hand on Paul's forearm. "If that's okay."

His expression softened. "Okay with me."

They began to whisper to each other, and Frank turned to me. "A recent couple—they're perfect for

60

our piece!" Then he lowered his voice. "And did you see how she lit up at the word 'couple'? Everyone needs *labels*. It's like no one's mature or secure enough."

"How do you know they're a recent couple?" I whispered, feeling peevish.

Frank chuckled. "I'm a journalist, Erica. It's my job to read body language. Check those two out." I looked at Paul and Katie as if seeing them for the first time. "See how they're staring into each other's eyes, their chairs almost on top of each other, her hand on his leg—"

"Yeah, you're right," I said, cutting him off. "I see." All of a sudden I was acutely aware of my hands on the table in front of me. Frank's were clasped in his lap. Hadn't we just started dating too? Why were we sitting so far apart? Why weren't we holding hands?

Duh, Erica, I told myself. *Have you forgotten the point of the Valentine's Day commentary section? That kind of thing is completely against everything you and Frank have talked about. PDAs, sap, gush. All that stuff makes us both sick?* So why was I suddenly wondering what it would be like to have it?

"Sounds like fun," Katie said, breaking my reverie. "Whenever you want to interview us is fine."

Paul nodded. "Name the time and place."

"Speaking of time and place," Frank said, turning to me, "there's a lecture tomorrow night that I thought you'd be interested in. One of my father's

61

friends, Dr. Muzacz, is a writing professor at Hopkins, and she's giving a talk on opinion writing in journalism. It could be a big help for the Valentine's edition."

"A college lecture?" I asked. I'd never stepped on college grounds, let alone attend a lecture at one. It sounded wonderfully mature.

"What other kind is there?" Frank asked. I laughed, then realized he wasn't kidding.

Paul rolled his eyes at me. I frowned back at him. "Of course I'd be interested. I'd love to go," I told Frank. Sure, journalism lectures weren't the kind of thing Paul and I did together when we hung out, but that didn't mean I couldn't appreciate one.

"Dr. Muzacz is going to discuss *All the President's Men*," Frank said. "It's the true story of two journalists who—"

"Yeah, I've heard of it," Paul said, flicking a crumb off the table.

"Hey, have you guys seen that new journalism movie yet?" Katie asked. "*Fit to Print*? It has an amazing soundtrack. My sister got the CD and—"

Frank scowled. "Dr. Muzacz is hardly going to discuss the *soundtrack* from *All the President's Men*. She'll be addressing the film's issues in an *intellectual* manner."

"I'm dying to see *Fit to Print*," I blurted out before Katie or Paul could say anything else about the film's music. I mean, please. Didn't they see that Frank was an artiste? That a film's music would not interest someone like him?

"I want to see it too," Katie jumped it. "Want to go see it together?"

I looked at Frank. He didn't look too enthusiastic.

Paul shrugged. "I don't know. We could, I guess."

"You're always saying you want me to get to know Erica," Katie reminded him. "This would be the perfect chance!"

"How about Saturday" I suggested. "Movie and dinner?" This would be a chance for my boyfriend and my best friend to get to know each other. Maybe Paul and Frank would find some common ground. Cheeseburgers. The Orioles. Monday Night Football. Something.

Plus, I'd get to know Katie. After all, if she was going to be a part of Paul's life, she was going to be a part of mine. Like it or not.

"Saturday it is," Katie declared. "Right, guys?"

"Righto," Paul mumbled.

Frank tilted his head. I took that as a yes.

A double date with Frank and Paul. I could hardly wait.

Five

"WHICH ONE?" I asked my little sister, holding up two sweaters. "I think I look older in the red one, but blue's a better color for me, right?"

Ellen glanced back and forth between them, folding her scrawny arms over her chest. Asking the most indecisive eleven-year-old in the world for advice was a bad move.

"Mom!" I yelled. "Mom, I need your help!"

"No, wait," Ellen insisted. "I can do this."

"Red or blue?" I held each under my face. "I can't believe I'm making such a big deal about this!"

"Why?" Ellen asked, sitting down next to me. "You're going on a date, aren't you? You're supposed to care how you look."

I smiled. Even my eleven-year-old sister understood more about dating than I did. "So make your decision. *Quick.*"

"The blue one," she announced.

I bit my lip. "Are you sure? Because this is a *college* lecture. You don't think the red makes me look older? More mature?"

Ellen rolled her eyes. "Fine. Wear the red one."

"But I thought you liked the—"

"Erica!" She jumped up, putting her hands on her hips. "Why did you even ask me?"

I sighed. "You're right. Okay. I'll just wear . . ." I closed my eyes and reached out to grab whichever sweater I touched first. I felt the soft fabric of the dark blue cardigan against my hand. "This one," I said, opening my eyes.

The phone meowed; I snatched up Garfield's head. "Hello?"

"Hey," Paul said. I looked at my sister, motioning for her to leave. She glared at me, and I mouthed a quick "thank you" before she ran out.

"Hi, what's up?" I dragged the phone back over to my bed. "I can't talk long," I told him, wiggling out of my jeans and reaching for the black pants I had picked out. "I have that lecture tonight with Frank."

"I know," Paul said. "The *college* lecture you haven't stopped talking about."

"Well, it's exciting for me," I said defensively, sucking in my stomach as I pulled the pants up and struggled with the buttons. The last time I'd worn those was definitely before I gave up doing crunches. I wished I could wear the black pants I'd bought a couple of weeks before, but I'd worn them on my first date with Frank.

"Well, I can't talk long either. I've got to start making some posters," Paul said.

"Posters?" I repeated, slipping a black belt through my belt loops.

"I meant to tell you the other day: I've decided to run for school historian."

"You what?" I exclaimed, sitting down hard on my bed. This had to be a bad dream.

"I know I need to get some more extracurricular stuff on my transcript, and I don't think I'm popular enough to win class president or anything," Paul said. "But I enjoy writing, and I'm great at record-keeping, so I thought historian would be up my alley." He laughed. "Besides, it's kind of a no guts, no glory position anyway. I mean, I probably won't even have any competition."

"Well . . ."

"But don't think I'm going to let you get out of helping me," Paul added. "I could use your amazing talents on the speech I'll have to make."

I gulped. "Paul . . . um . . . actually you're going to have some competition."

"Who? You?" Paul kidded.

"No. Frank."

Silence. "Great," Paul finally said. "I should have guessed."

"I can't exactly help both of you," I said slowly.

"Well, I'm sure Frank will understand," Paul said. "I mean you and I go back a long ways, and—"

"I already promised Frank I'd help him," I said,

feeling sick to my stomach. "I can't go back now and tell him I'm helping you instead."

"What do you even see in him?" Paul snapped. "Really, I don't get it. You're gonna tell me you thought the way he acted the other day was cool?"

"You're right," I said angrily. "You don't get it. You don't get that Frank is mature. He thinks about things intellectually. And I'm beginning to think more like that too."

"Then that's your loss."

"I guess," I said tartly.

Paul sighed.

Then I sighed. "I really am sorry about the campaign," I said. "You know I'd do it for you in a second if things were different."

"I know," he said. "Don't worry about it. Just have fun tonight and fill me in tomorrow."

"I will." I hesitated. "And thanks for, well, for understanding."

"Bye, Erica."

"Bye." I hung up the phone, my hand resting on Garfield's body for a few moments. I felt horrible about not helping Paul. But I couldn't. He'd asked me second.

And I wanted to help Frank. I wanted to impress him. Wanted to work closely with him on something outside of the *Postscript*. I wished I could help both of them, but I doubted either of them would be into that. They were running *against* each other.

I sat down at my vanity table and rooted through

my makeup bag. A little mascara, a little blush, a little lip gloss. I brushed my hair, then thought about winding it up into a sophisticated bun. That seemed too much, though.

"Erica," my mom called up the stairs, "Frank's here."

I grabbed the blue sweater and pulled it over my head, then stared into the mirror. There was no way I'd be mistaken for a college freshman. Would I be the youngest person there? Maybe I should stay home.

Stop it, I told myself. *If you were going to this lecture with Paul, you wouldn't be worrying about anything. You're just as comfortable with Frank as you are with Paul. It's simply that you feel stuff for Frank you've never felt for Paul. That's the only reason you're so nervous.*

It's normal to be this nervous and worried around someone, right? Isn't that how you're supposed to feel?

"In closing," Professor Muzacz droned on, looking at her note cards, "how strongly to voice your opinions in a journalistic medium is worthy of intense consideration, since the consequences of what you express can in fact be far-reaching."

She finally stepped back from the podium, and the audience applauded, so I began clapping too. Frank was beaming with admiration and smacking his hands together really loudly.

"Isn't she incredible?" Frank exclaimed as we

stood up and followed the others into the adjoining room, where snacks and beverages were being served. We were the only high-school students there, although Frank could easily have passed for a college guy in his black slacks and wool crewneck sweater.

"Yeah, that was a pretty amazing speech," I replied, though I was amazed only by how boring the speaker had been. She'd been really dry, and she'd read from her note cards for most of her talk. But Frank seemed so impressed that I didn't think he'd appreciate my real reaction.

I was relieved to see food and drinks set up on little tables. I picked up one of the small plastic plates and filled it with fresh fruit from a carved-out watermelon. I'd skipped dinner, since I'd been too nervous to eat before the date, and as soon as I popped the first strawberry in my mouth I realized I was starving.

Is it okay to eat a lot of this stuff? I wondered as I watched Frank putting a couple of pieces of fruit and a few crackers on his plate. Probably not, or they would have provided larger plates. I tried to keep from drooling as I caught sight of a tray stacked with every imaginable kind of cookie.

"There are some people I want you to meet," Frank whispered, guiding me toward a group of adults. *At least we're getting closer to the cookies,* I thought, nervous about being introduced to these professor types.

"Professor Grassi." Frank put his hand on a tall, balding man's shoulder.

"Frank London!" the older man exclaimed. He turned to the people he'd been talking to. "Frank is a high-school student who took a college-level journalism summer session with me," he explained. "He wrote some truly outstanding pieces."

I tried to keep my eyes from bulging. Frank had managed to amaze a college professor? Wow.

"Well, you know what they say." Frank smiled, not even blinking at a compliment that would have reduced me to a babbling moron. "Half of it is having a teacher who can bring it out in you."

The professor and his group chuckled. "So who's your friend?" he asked Frank, smiling at me.

Please don't blush, I begged myself, already feeling the color rising in my cheeks.

"This is Erica Park," Frank announced, putting his arm around me and pulling me closer to their group.

"Erica's my new coeditor at our high-school paper," he continued. "You should see her articles—she's incredibly talented." The not-blushing thing was now officially impossible.

Professor Grassi raised an eyebrow. "Praise from Frank? You must be quite a writer."

"I—I hope so." *Lame,* I chided myself.

"So, did you enjoy Professor Muzacz's lecture?" the professor asked us.

"Absolutely fascinating," Frank proclaimed. While he discussed how her ideas would help him form an article he was working on, my attention was diverted to the cookie tray.

I slipped away, which seemed okay because I'd already heard about this article. At the cookie table, I debated between chocolate chip and chocolate chocolate chip. *Oh, what the heck,* I thought, grabbing two of each and stacking them on a napkin.

When I returned to Frank's side, munching happily, he was still talking about the article. I gazed around, glimpsing a couple who stood very close together in a corner. The guy was feeding her a cracker covered with cheese off his plate. The girl grinned and opened her mouth in a cute way.

Couples who fed each other in public—another dating ritual for my article. She got most of the cracker in her mouth, but some of the cheese fell onto the floor, and they both giggled. He bent down to retrieve the hunk of cheese, wrapping it in a napkin and leaving it on the table next to them. Then he inched the cracker close to her lips, grinning at her.

So this kind of stuff *wasn't* limited to high school. *That* was interesting.

They were clearly either in love or falling in love. And they seemed to be having a lot of fun.

Yeah, having fun making fools *of themselves,* I told myself. Just because I was beginning to understand why couples acted like that didn't mean it still wasn't sort of tacky, right?

I mean, I couldn't see Frank feeding me a cracker full of cheese even in private.

I turned my attention back to him. He was chuckling over something the professor was saying. *He's so comfortable among these people,* I noted, my gaze riveted by the lock of blond hair on his forehead. *He's so self-assured and confident and smart. Not to mention gorgeous.*

"It was nice meeting you, Erica," the professor suddenly said, extending a hand toward me. I quickly chewed the big bite of cookie I had in my mouth.

"You too!" I said, shaking his hand. As Frank watched them head off, his expression seemed full of admiration. I realized I'd never really seen him look that way before. This was clearly his element.

"How are the cookies?" Frank asked.

"Really good," I said, swallowing.

"I'm surprised they served cookies," Frank said, reaching out his hand to brush something away from the corner of my mouth. "Crumbs," he explained with a smile. "This kind of crowd usually sticks with fruit, cheese, and crackers."

Darn. I *knew* I shouldn't have gone for those cookies. Frank was so good at this sort of thing. He knew how to act, what to say, when to laugh, when to listen. I felt like such a *kid*.

"So, why don't we head out?" he suggested. "We can walk back to town through the park."

I nodded, and we walked down the long corridor and out the front doors. "Look at that!" I exclaimed, awestruck by the shadowy, scary patterns the limbs of the big old oak tree were making on the grass.

"It's almost like dancing monsters!" Paul loved when things made funny silhouettes; he could stare at clouds and trees and people's shadows forever.

"It's so cute that you're into that," Frank said.

Once again I felt like such a kid. Cookies, monsters . . . maybe I should see if Frank wanted to come over and watch "Sesame Street." It was true—I wasn't as mature and sophisticated as Frank. And when he realized that, would he decide he didn't like me after all?

"So that professor seems to think you're great," I said, walking faster to keep up with Frank.

"I loved his course. You should enroll this coming summer. I know he'd be thrilled to have another student who can actually put a sentence together."

"Really? Me?" I grinned and bit my lip. A college-level journalism class? That would be so awesome! Especially if there were other high-school kids in the class, I realized. But why would a high-schooler take a summer course at a college anyway?

Frank didn't appear to think too highly of anyone, but he seemed to think of me as his equal. Weird. Just two weeks earlier, that alone would have had me spinning in total happiness. But for some reason it didn't. Half of me loved that he respected me. But half of me didn't love that he never had anything nice to say about anyone.

He stopped suddenly. "I'm so glad you came tonight," he said softly, reaching out to touch my cheek. "And I'm really looking forward to seeing you and your friends tomorrow night for *Fit to Print*."

Beat-beat-beat. Ping-ping-ping.

His fingers brushed my skin. He stepped closer to me.

Closer.

Was he going to kiss me?

He leaned that gorgeous face close to mine, and all thoughts went straight out of my brain. Those warring halves of me suddenly fused together, loving *everything* about him.

His lips pressed against mine and I closed my eyes. When he pulled away, I stumbled slightly backward, light-headed, dizzy.

When I opened my eyes, Frank was smiling sweetly at me.

"That's so *cute*," he said. "You acted like that was your first kiss."

Cute.

Great. Now he thinks I've never been kissed before! Would I ever feel prepared enough for him?

He started walking again, and I hurried to keep up. I kept expecting him to hold my hand, but his hands never left his pockets.

I guess I was right about Frank London. Even in private, he just wasn't a PDA kind of guy.

And wasn't that what I claimed to want?

Six

"THAT'S SO *CUTE*," Frank commented as Paul and Katie slid into the same side of the booth at the T-Bone Diner. Frank and I had no choice but to sit next to each other across from them. It was romantic, I guess, but it just didn't feel comfortable.

Paul shot me a look, which I ignored. I suddenly became very interested in the soup of the day on the specials section of the menu.

This sitting-next-to-each-other thing was another example of bizarre couple behavior for my article, which I bizarrely hadn't really worked on much at all. *Why* wasn't I delighting in writing down all these silly couple things? Like the way Paul had fed Katie popcorn all during *Fit to Print*. The way she'd leaned her head against his shoulder. The way he hadn't let go of her hand since we left the movie theater and walked next door to the diner.

"You've been here, right?" I asked Frank. The T-Bone Diner was a big Emerson High hangout, but I couldn't remember ever spotting him there during one of my pig-out trips with Paul, or with Linda and Sharon.

"Diners aren't really my thing," Frank said, picking up his oversized menu. "I prefer restaurants. But I know diners are big with high-school students. It's really *cute,* actually."

Katie and Paul exchanged a look. The fake smile plastered on Paul's face wasn't going to last much longer. I knew him too well.

"Frank took me to this *really* elegant Italian place last weekend," I told them. Somehow I felt I needed to explain, to make them understand that his tastes were just more refined than ours. What was so terrible about that? Why couldn't they see how mature Frank was?

Katie nodded; Paul started studying his menu. Frank was scanning his own menu with that same adorable concentration he used whenever he read anything. Suddenly the kiss popped into my mind. Or *kisses,* I should say. The night before, he'd walked me home, then kissed me again in front of my house. I'd tried not to act as though it were such a big deal the second time around.

But it had been.

This was our third official date. Frank was definitely on his way to becoming my boyfriend.

"So, Frank, what did you think of *Fit to Print?*"

Paul asked as he closed the menu. I shot Paul a warning glance, recognizing that edge of antagonism in his voice.

Frank sighed, closing his menu and brushing his hair out of his face. "It was okay—for that type of movie."

Katie wrinkled her nose. "What do you mean?" she asked. *Is it me, or did they manage to scrunch even closer together?* I wondered.

"Well, you can't expect the Hollywood version of journalism to be very accurate, right?"

"But the story was decent," Paul cut in, placing his elbows on the table and leaning forward.

Frank chuckled. "The *story* was total cheese." He shook his head. "Nothing like the good old story about how boy meets girl, thinks he hates her, then realizes he loves her and manages to win a Pulitzer prize on the side, right?"

I giggled and smiled at Frank. Then I saw the scowl on Paul's face. "Oh, come on," I argued. "Even you have to admit that the sap factor of that movie was off the charts."

Paul met my eyes, and I mentally pleaded with him to just let it drop.

"So, do we all know what we're having?" he asked.

I sighed, fiddling with my fork. If anything, Paul and Frank had less tolerance for each other than ever before.

"Hey, kids, whatcha want?"

Paul grinned at me. Our favorite waitress had her pencil poised over her order pad.

Maxi wore a ton of makeup and very revealing clothes. Paul and I loved her. Frank glanced up and did a double take, then turned to me, smiling and rolling his eyes.

"Cheeseburger and chocolate shake," Paul said.

"The same but vanilla," I said.

Katie giggled. "The same but chocolate and cheese on the fries too."

Frank slapped his menu shut. "The low-cal fruit plate and an iced tea." He lowered his voice. "You guys should really lay off the red meat and cheese. It's like signing a death wish."

"I'll keep it in mind," Paul said dryly. He turned to Maxi. "And make that rare please."

"Coming up, kids," Maxi said, writing down the order with a flourish.

After that, Paul and Katie started having their own private little conversation, so Frank and I started discussing the movie and how it related to the professor's lecture the previous night. It was as though the four of us were two separate couples who didn't know each other and had been stuck sharing a table.

"Here you go, kids," Maxi announced, setting down three chocolate milkshakes and Frank's iced tea. I stared at the shake in front of me, then darted a glance at Paul. He hesitated, as though he was waiting for Frank to notice that the waitress had gotten my order wrong. Anyone who knew me knew I loved vanilla milkshakes. And that I wasn't good at telling waitresses, even ones I knew, that they'd given me the wrong thing.

Frank took a big sip of his iced tea.

"Maxi?" Paul called as she walked away.

She turned back. "What's up, hon?"

"Uh, you know how much Park here likes vanilla shakes, Maxi," Paul said. "*I'm* the chocoholic."

She grinned at me and slid the shake to Paul's side of the table. "Then you have this one too, on me," she said. "I'll be right back with your shake, Erica."

"She *could* have apologized," Frank commented. "She can forget getting a good tip."

"Maxi's a great waitress," Paul said, picking up his shake. He looked annoyed.

"She's a friend of ours," I added hastily. I knew Frank thought he was standing up for me. Couldn't Paul see that?

Frank rolled his eyes. "Whatever. Anyway, Paul, have you been working on your speech for the historian debate?"

"Hmm-mmm," Paul replied. "I've got a pretty good first draft. I've been working on it for a while."

"Done," Frank said. "I wrote *mine* between classes yesterday."

"See, I've got to hand it to you," Paul said. I shot him a nervous glance. "It's gotta be tough not to come up with a piece of junk for a speech when you're scribbling it during period breaks." He smiled innocently.

Frank's eyes narrowed. "Not if you're a writer."

I sighed, officially giving up hope that Paul and Frank could get along.

We were all relieved when our dinners were

served. We didn't have to talk. We could occupy ourselves with stuffing our faces.

It amazed me that Paul and Katie were still snuggled up against each other and nuzzling, even while eating cheeseburgers and fries. Another person entirely could fit in the space between Frank and me. Did that mean something too? Maybe he didn't like me?

Don't forget that incredible kiss and all the really nice things he's said to you. Of course he likes you. PDAs are just not his style. They didn't used to be yours either. Until you hooked up with Frank.

Finally we all finished up, and when Maxi dropped off the check, we pounced on it as if it were the key to let us out of a jail cell.

"Why don't I just put this on my MasterCard, and the rest of you can give me cash?" Frank suggested, half standing as he pulled his wallet out of the back pocket of his khakis.

Katie's and Paul's mouths dropped open, sort of the way mine almost had at La Dolce Vita. Then they exchanged another of those what's-his-deal looks, probably the millionth one of the night. Okay, so it was pretty strange that a guy our age had a credit card, but did they have to be so hard on him just because he was more mature than the rest of us?

"This place doesn't take credit cards," Paul said with a hint of triumph in his voice.

Frank paled a little, and he looked at me, his mouth twitching. "Uh . . ."

"I owe you some money anyway," I jumped in,

guessing that he didn't have anything on him but plastic. I was *not* going to let Paul think Frank was sticking me with paying for him.

"Hold on a sec," I said, unzipping my purse and digging around for my Hello Kitty wallet, which was yet another spoof gift from Paul. "Here," I said, thrusting the money onto the table. I refused to meet Paul's eyes.

We counted out the right amount, and Paul put in enough for him and Katie, then Frank scooped it all up and walked to the cash register.

"I'm just going to run to the rest room," Katie said, jumping up and letting go of Paul's hand.

As soon as we were alone, I turned to Paul with a furious expression.

"What is your problem?" I hissed. "Why are you being such a jerk?"

"Me?" Paul cried, his eyes widening. "What about your boyfriend?"

"First of all, he's not my boyfriend," I said. "Yet. But I'm *hoping* that will change. Why can't you give him a chance? I'm trying to be nice to Katie, right?"

"That's not difficult," Paul shot back.

"Well, I haven't said a single sarcastic thing *despite* the fact that you and Katie were practically *glued* to each other's side!" I realized I was almost shouting, and lowered my voice. "Why can't you just be *happy* for me?" I asked.

"I just . . ." He paused, glanced in Frank's direction, then back at me. "I just don't think he's the right guy for you. But . . . I don't know, I mean . . .

maybe I wouldn't think anyone was, you know?"

I stared at him, shocked. Why was that the most comforting thing I'd heard all night? I was so relieved that he still seemed to have special feelings for me. But why?

He was the same old Paul he'd always been. My best friend. The guy I'd known better than anyone forever. The guy who knew me better than anyone. The guy I'd never, ever have to be nervous around.

"Look, forget that," he said. "Just—okay, here it is. I'm never gonna be Frank's big fan, all right? But I promise to *try* to deal with him as long as he's making you happy."

I smiled. "Thank you. And I promise not to roll my eyes too much when I see you and Katie playing Twister without the mat."

"Does that—are you actually bothered by the me-and-Katie thing?" A strange, intense gleam flickered in his eyes. "Or are all the PDAs just grossing you out as usual? I'd have thought you'd changed your mind about PDAs now that you're *in love*. But from the looks of things between you two, I guess not."

It was like I'd been hit by a Mack truck or something. He'd said too much in that one breath for me to respond to, and I didn't even know the answers.

"Hey, sorry it took so long." I jerked my head up and saw Katie standing at the edge of our table. She was smiling at Paul, but there was something in her eyes that made the smile seem forced.

Paul stood up, encircling her with his arm and pulling her against his side.

Frank strode back to the table. "Well, I guess we're done here."

We all smiled.

I flopped on my bed and pulled the comforter over me, my notebook on my stomach. I *had* to start writing my Valentine's Day article. But I couldn't concentrate, couldn't figure out what had happened to my big stance on the holiday.

The scary thing was, I'd started dreaming about what I'd be getting from Frank for Valentine's Day.

After we'd left the diner earlier, Paul and Katie had turned left; Frank and I had turned right. He'd walked me home, our conversation centering on the movie we'd all seen, which Frank hated. He didn't say anything negative about the date itself, which I thought was really cool of him.

My toes started tingling from the memory of the kiss. We'd stood in front of my house, gazing at each other. Then, before I knew what was happening, he cupped his hand under my chin and leaned closer, gently pressing his lips to mine.

Everything inside me turned to mush. His arms wrapped around me as he deepened the kiss. . . .

Garfield meowed, jolting me out of the memory. I jumped out of bed to grab the phone, hoping to hear Frank's deep voice wishing me sweet dreams.

"Hey."

"Hi, Paul."

"Listen, I'm really sorry about tonight."

"It's okay," I told him distractedly. "So maybe

you and Frank weren't meant to be best buds."

"Are *you* okay?"

"I'm great," I chirped. Paul knew me well enough to figure out that whenever I sounded like a bird, I wasn't great at all.

"Oh, good. So anyway, tell me what you thought of Katie. I really want your opinion."

That was strange. He hadn't even *noticed* my parakeet voice?

"She seems really nice," I said, which was true. "I didn't get to talk to her much."

"Want to hang out with us tomorrow afternoon?" he asked. "You could get to know her better. I think you two would really like each other."

They were seeing each other two days in a row? That was serious. "Tomorrow?" I stalled; I had plans to help Frank work on his campaign in the evening, but I didn't really want to bring that up. "What time?"

"Around two? I'm gonna take her to the Bowl-a-Rama."

I blinked. "Oh." Somehow that felt weird, Paul taking Katie to our hangout. "Katie likes to bowl?" I asked. I wondered if Frank ever went bowling. So far we hadn't talked about much besides journalism.

"Uh, actually, she doesn't." He paused. "I mean, she's never really done it much, is all. But I figured we'd just hang out in Bowl-a-Rama's arcade and try some skee ball."

I grinned. "And you really want me to whip your butt in front of Katie?"

"Ex*cuse* me? I'm the reigning champ in this

friendship, Park, and—" There was a click on the phone. "Oh, hold on a sec."

I waited while Paul answered his call waiting.

"Hey, Erica? Katie's on the other line. I've gotta go."

"Oh. Okay," I said.

But I was shocked. Paul had never hung up on me for anyone. *It's different now,* I reminded myself. *And that's a good thing.*

"I'll see you tomorrow," Paul continued. "You can meet us there, right?"

I bit my lip. "Uh-huh."

"Okay, see ya then."

He clicked off.

I stared at the receiver.

Another girl had taken my place with Paul.

Erica: Do you have any special Valentine's Day memories?

Sharon: I wish. I've never had a Valentine. Well, except for my mom, but I don't think that really counts.

Erica: But you've dated plenty of guys. Why is Valentine's Day so important?

Sharon: Oh, come on, Er, it's a *huge* deal. You have to watch all the other girls with their candygrams and stuffed animals, and then the couples who get all gooey with each other. The worst is seeing the guy you're in love with giving all that stuff to his girlfriend. Alex broke up with me in January last year, and then on Valentine's Day I walk into English and there's his new girlfriend with this big thing of flowers from him. That was major pain.

Erica: Okay, so maybe we should focus on the future. What are your plans for this Valentine's Day?

Sharon: I have to find a date for the dance so that I don't feel like a total loser. But trust me, the hardest thing about that day is watching the guy you want with another girl.

Seven

PAUL WAS HUNCHED over a pinball machine, and Katie was standing at his side, cheering. Her cream-colored pants and black knit sweater made her look way too delicate for the place. I glanced down at my jeans and long-sleeved navy T-shirt, feeling kind of underdressed next to her. "Hi, guys."

"Wait just a . . . ," Paul muttered, desperately hitting the buttons to keep the little metal ball in action. "Arrgh. I bombed! Oh, well, Katie's not into pinball anyway."

I glanced at Katie. "It gives me a headache," she admitted.

"Now that you're here we can play skee ball," Paul said. I noticed a flicker of nervousness in Katie's eyes.

"It's really not that hard," I told her as we followed Paul into the back of the arcade.

She smiled gratefully and moved a little closer to

me. "I've never been to this kind of place before," she whispered. "But I guess that's pretty obvious. Lee warned me to be careful where I sit down in these pants."

Paul had introduced her to Lee? I felt another stab of that same weird hurt. Lee was *my* friend, mine and Paul's, and he was already giving Katie advice on how to avoid a dry-cleaning bill?

Stop being silly, I scolded myself. Lee talked to plenty of people besides Paul and me. So what if Katie was one of them now?

"Here we are," Paul said, taking Katie's hand. "See—it looks like a little bowling lane, right?" She nodded. "Only you're not trying to knock anything down, you're just trying to sink the balls in those holes with the most points. Got it?"

She nodded, glancing nervously at me. Was she afraid of making a fool of herself in front of Paul? *She must really, really like him,* I thought.

"Let's do a test game together," Paul suggested. He slipped a token in the machine, then stood behind Katie and held her arm, guiding her through the motions of swinging the ball.

I shifted back and forth on my feet, biting my lip as I observed the gentle way Paul cradled Katie's arm while he took her through the steps of the game.

He was so sweet. So patient. So affectionate.

So good-looking.

Wait a minute. Where did that thought come from?

Yes, Paul was good-looking. But he'd always

been good-looking in the same way the sky was blue; it was just a fact. So why was I noticing it in a different way?

It's just because he's here with Katie and you're seeing him the way she sees him. That makes total sense.

I tried to imagine being there with Frank, but I couldn't picture us being all affectionate the way Paul and Katie were.

Finally Katie seemed to have the hang of it, and I moved over to my own lane next to Paul. For the first few minutes Paul kept stopping his game to help her out, but soon he got caught up in playing and we started our usual competitive battle.

"Check that out!" I jabbed Paul in the shoulder and pointed at the 520 on my scoreboard.

"How'd you do that?" he asked in amazement.

"I got five hundreds!" I announced proudly.

"Okay, now you're in for it," Paul told me, grinning.

"I'm gonna take a break," Katie cut in. "There's a kid over there waiting for this lane, and I'm kind of thirsty anyway."

Paul glanced at me, then back at Katie. "Uh, okay," he said. "Do you want us to come?"

"No," she assured him. "I'll be right back. I'm just gonna grab a soda."

"Okay." Paul looked relieved. He gave her a kiss on the cheek and then she walked away.

Paul and I resumed our games, and soon we were laughing and joking around again. "Shoot, I'm out of tokens," I said.

He reached into his pocket and pulled out two tokens, dropping them down on the ledge between our lanes. "These are my last ones," he told me. "We'll split 'em."

I smiled. At least *some* traditions were still just ours, like playing the last game together. We took turns rolling the balls, watching each other's shots.

"We're tied!" I announced.

"Wow! We equally rule!" Paul gave me a big hug, and I threw my arms around his neck, giggling. He spun me around, lifting my feet off the floor. We both laughed so hard we almost toppled over. But then, all of a sudden, he let go of me and stepped back.

I turned around, and there was Katie, watching us with a just-about-to-crumple face. Paul took a step toward her, but she ran toward the snack bar.

"Let me talk to her," I said to Paul. "I can explain this."

He nodded, and I chased after her.

She sat on a stool at the snack bar, shredding a napkin. She looked like she was about to cry.

"Katie," I said softly, sitting down next to her, "I know that must have looked weird, but—"

"Erica," she interrupted, "I know you guys are just friends. Paul's told me that." The expression in her eyes was definitely in the danger zone, but moving out of red alert for waterworks. "But the way he talks about you, and the way you guys act together . . ."

I shook my head. "We've known each other since the days when playing in mud puddles was a major life activity," I explained. "So we just—I mean, we

92

have this overly natural way of communicating, like we're in each other's brain sometimes. And that's how I know he's totally crazy about you."

She turned to face me. "Really?" she asked.

"Yeah, really. You should *see* the way he lights up when he talks about you. Katie, you've made him so happy." I stiffened, not sure why. Maybe all this sappy talk was affecting my brain. "There is *nothing* for you to worry about, believe me."

Yeah, because Paul's got this new habit of dropping me—even literally now—whenever you call or show up.

"I should go apologize," Katie said. "Thanks, Erica. I feel like such an idiot."

"No problem," I assured her. So why did I suddenly feel like the one who needed comforting?

She jumped off the stool. "Aren't you coming?"

"Um, I don't think so," I answered. "I have to be at Frank's pretty soon. Tell Paul bye for me, okay?"

She nodded. "Thanks again."

Even though I was off to see Frank, I felt depressed as I left the Bowl-a-Rama. Paul had brought Katie to our hangout, into our world, and she didn't even *like* it there. How could anyone not love skee ball, pinball, and bowling?

More important, how could Paul really like any girl who didn't?

Ah . . . choo! Ugh. How mortifying was it to sneeze—a huge, loud, horrible sneeze—in front of Frank! *Ah . . . chooooooooo!*

He continued to type away at his laptop. We were in his bedroom, which was spotless—unless you counted the mess I'd made with poster paper, crayons, glue, and glitter on the carpet by his bed. Either his mom was a major cleaner or Frank was really, really, really neat. It was so cool to be in his house, in his room. I thought I might learn something more about him, from the posters on his wall or the favorite things he kept around, but there was only the usual bedroom stuff and a few books on journalism.

Ah . . . choo!

No *bless you.* No acknowledgment. Good. Maybe he hadn't even heard me. That was Frank— he was so focused, so dedicated, so deeply passionate about his work. And he was adding the finishing touches to his campaign speech, so I wasn't surprised he was lost in thought. But there was a box of tissues two inches from his hand, on top of a stack of papers on his desk. *Oh, no . . . another one is—*

Ah . . . choooooooo! "Can I have a tissue, please?" I asked him.

No response.

"Frank? A tissue?" I repeated.

He grabbed the box and tossed it to me without even turning around.

"Thanks." I pulled out a few tissues, acutely aware of how loudly I was blowing my nose. This was so embarrassing! But talk about *silly.* I mean, I'd have expected Linda to be worried about gross sneezes in front of her boyfriend. But me? Paul would have laughed in my face if he'd been able to read my mind just then. I must have sneezed in front of him a thousand million times over the past nine years—without a shred of embarrassment.

This was exactly the kind of thing I had planned to make fun of in my anti–Valentine's Day article. Linda and a lot of other girls would run out of the dance in horror if they started sneezing like this in front of the guy they liked. I would have thought that was the stupidest thing in the world. Before Frank. I just hoped I wasn't coming down with a cold—Valentine's Day was only six days away.

I turned my attention back to the campaign poster I was working on. I wasn't much of an artist—glue, sparkles, and glitter were everywhere. The only medium I had mastered was the crayons.

"So, how's the editing of your speech going?" I asked his back.

"Uh-huh," he answered.

I sighed. When Frank had asked me for help with his campaign, the last thing I'd expected was to be sitting on his bedroom floor with gold specks glued to my thumb. I'd pictured myself working on the speech, using my *mind* rather than my clearly ineffectual hands.

Like Frank London really needs you to help him write something. That would be like Salvador Dali asking someone like . . . well, me to help him paint. Although I guess you could say my posters were coming out with a sort of surrealist spin to them.

Suddenly Frank pushed back his chair and spun around. "I have to make a phone call," he said.

"Could you check this for me?" He gestured at the laptop's screen.

My heart jumped. He *did* want my advice.

I stood up, brushing various art supplies off me and onto the paper towels covering his carpet. He glanced down at my little disaster area and wrinkled his nose.

"What did you do?" he asked in a horrified voice.

My cheeks flamed. "I, uh, it's sort of a work in progress," I said lamely. "I mean, a few works in . . . progress."

Frank shrugged. "Whatever. I'll be back in a few, okay?"

I nodded, relieved that he didn't seem too upset. I sat down at his desk in front of the laptop. The spell-check box was in the center of the screen. *Oh.* He really meant *check* in, like, the most menial sense of the word.

I mechanically hit the keys as the spell-check did its thing. Boy, did I feel *not* important as I told the computer whether to replace or ignore all of Frank's mongo-huge vocabulary words. Would anyone in our class even understand a word he was saying?

I'd finished when Frank came back, and I wondered if I should mention anything about his word choices. I didn't want him to think *I* couldn't follow him. Even though I was pretty sure by this time that Frank really liked me, I still got nervous about doing something that would give away the fact that I wasn't at his level.

"Thanks," he said, standing behind me and rubbing

my shoulders. He leaned his head down next to my ear. "I really appreciate all your help."

Okay, saying anything at the moment was a definite impossibility with all those sparks igniting everywhere in my body.

At that very moment I sneezed. *Great. Just when he's touching me. Really romantic, Erica!*

"Uh, Frank? Could you hand me that box of tissues again?" He snatched up the box and gave it to me, then sat on the edge of his bed, facing me. I quickly blew my nose again. "I skimmed over your speech while I was doing the spell-check."

"Pretty good, huh?" He stared at me intently, as if my opinion was really important to him.

"It was *great,* of course," I began. Frank nodded. "But I did think maybe you should tone down some of the language a little."

He frowned. "Tone it down?"

I immediately regretted saying anything. Now Frank would think I was stupid on top of a sneezing slob.

"Well, I guess you're right," he acknowledged. I let out my breath. "I tend to forget that the IQs of most of our classmates are in no danger of breaking into triple digits."

I bit my lip. *That* was harsh. "Well, no, that wasn't exactly what I meant," I said carefully. "It's not about people being dumb or not getting it. It's more that not everyone is as into the nitty-gritty of facts as you are, so you want to explain your great ideas in a way that will *interest* them—not make them look for the nearest dictionary."

Frank nodded. "That's good advice. It's funny, you sound just like Doug—he's always telling me I need to take my writing down a few levels." He was staring at me. "I'm so lucky to have you on my side." The intensity of his gaze was almost too much; I glanced away, then back at him. I'd definitely impressed him if I was saying the same thing Mr. Serson was.

I am definitely the lucky one, I thought as he moved forward to kiss me, brushing a piece of glitter out of my hair. *I am one lucky, artistically challenged girl.*

Ah . . . choooooooo!

Eight

"THIS SUCKS," I declared as I turned off the television. I had spent all day watching talk shows and soap operas, and I'd finally reached my limit.

Of course I had to get sick on a day when Charlie and Ellen both have after-school activities, I thought miserably. At that point I could have even gone for playing video games with my brother. At least it would have been some three-dimensional human contact.

I reached for a tissue from the nearly empty box just as the phone rang. I scrambled up off the sofa and ran into the kitchen to answer it.

"Heddo?" Man, stuffed noses were so annoying.

"Hi, Erica?"

Frank!

He'd obviously noticed I hadn't gone to school that day and was calling to see how I was feeling! How sweet was that?

"You've got a cold?" he asked.

"Yeah. I woke up this morning and I could barely breathe." I sank into one of the kitchen chairs, propping my elbows up on the table.

"Oh, that's right—you were sneezing a lot yesterday," he said. "How are you feeling now?"

"A little better, I guess." I blew my nose again.

"That's good. So, you think you'll be in school tomorrow?"

He *did* miss me! Already the pain of my sore, too-frequently-blown nose was fading.

"I think so," I said. "But my cold's pretty bad."

"Oh. It's just that I could definitely use a few more posters for my campaign. I put up the ones you made yesterday, but your friend Paul has some really professional ones up. So, if you're gonna be back in school and you're not that sick, maybe you could work on some new ones tomorrow afternoon."

Paul had professional-looking campaign posters? Huh?

"Oh, and I called a quick *Postscript* meeting today," he continued. "Dale quit the paper over something stupid, so I've assigned his article to you, if that's okay. Something related to Emerson's music program will be fine."

"Uh . . . yeah. No problem." Why was he talking to me like I was still an assistant instead of his coeditor? *It's not his fault you were sick today and missed their meeting,* I told myself. Frank just didn't have time to do the article himself, and he obviously trusted me with it more than anyone else, which was a compliment, really.

"Great," he said. "That'll be a huge help. And how's your work on the Valentine's stuff coming?"

"Great," I lied. For some reason I'd had this strange creative block for over a week. I hadn't interviewed anyone else. I hadn't written anything. It was kind of hard to stay so cynical now that I was a member of the lovesick population myself. That was why I hadn't set up that interview with Paul and Katie. It was really hard to watch my own best friend do all the mushy, sappy things I wished Frank would do.

But I'd have bet anything that Frank's own views had started changing too. I mean, how could they not, with those mind-blowing kisses we'd shared? And what better way to make him aware of it, or at least acknowledge it, than by interviewing *him*? "Um . . . Frank, I'd really like to interview you for my Valentine's article."

"If I have time, sure," he said. "I'm really looking forward to the dance on Saturday night. We'll get great material."

"I know!" I replied, instantly cheering up at the thought of the dance. *Great material for how we ourselves have changed!* "And I'm looking forward to it too." I had a feeling that after that dance Frank and I would finally be a couple, like, for *real*. We pretty much already were, but it wasn't official. I hadn't wanted to bring anything up, because I knew how Frank felt about labels. But if *I* wanted to call him my boyfriend, he probably wanted to call me his girlfriend.

101

Frank London, my boyfriend.

"I've got to go study for a test," Frank continued. "See you tomorrow."

"See you tomorrow," I echoed, aware of the dreamy smile on my face.

The doorbell rang the second I hung up.

I peeked through the curtain covering the glass window on the door. Paul.

He wouldn't care that I looked like a total disaster, would he? He'd seen me looking worse than this countless times. I checked myself out in the mirror by the door; I looked pretty bad, but there wasn't much I could do about it.

It's just Paul, I told myself. *What's your problem?* Maybe it was that Katie always looked so great, so pulled-together.

I opened the door; Paul smiled at me. "I've got your complete get-well package," he announced, gesturing at the huge shopping bag he carried. He followed me to the living room and plopped down on the sofa, setting the bag on the coffee table. He peered at my face closely. Suddenly I wished I didn't look so ugly.

"Your eyes look okay," he said. "So there's probably no fever, right?"

I nodded, grinning at his amateur diagnosis. "It's just my nose," I explained, dropping down next to him on the couch. "It's driving me crazy."

Paul stuck his arm into the bag and pulled out a box of tissues and a can of chicken noodle soup. "These should help." He placed them on the coffee table. "And the tissues have that lotion stuff, so they won't hurt your nose."

I shook my head, marveling at how perfect his gifts were. "Paul, thank you so much! That's exactly what I need."

"Well, you probably don't need this." He pulled out a pile of papers and plopped them down between us. "I went around to your teachers to collect your homework, since I know you hate getting behind. But before you worry about that, there's entertainment." He whipped out a video—*Grease*, one of our favorites.

"Oh, that's great!" I exclaimed. "Is there popcorn in your little bag of treats too?" I asked eagerly.

"Sorry." Paul shook his head, his eyes twinkling. "That's not good for you."

I groaned. "Come on, Doc, it's just a little cold."

He put his hand on my forehead, clearly to check my temperature. "It's more than that, sickie."

I swatted his hand away, but between the cold medicine I'd taken and the sudden movement, I lurched forward right onto him. He reached his hands out to steady me, holding my arms. Our faces were just inches apart, and we just looked at each other, not saying anything, not laughing, not even smiling. I had a strange urge to smooth down that little tuft of hair that stuck up at the back of his head. A strange urge to . . .

Beat-beat-beat. Ping-ping-ping.

Huh? What's going on in there? This is Paul. Paul. My best friend.

103

I swallowed and moved back a bit. "Uh, sorry," I murmured.

He stared at me for one more moment. "Do you always attack your doctors?" He was attempting a joke, but he wasn't smiling, and his voice had a high pitch to it. "So . . . I should actually be going," he said, kicking at the rug.

He felt it too. Otherwise he'd be sliding *Grease* in the VCR, heating up the soup, and telling me a funny story about something that happened at lunch.

Something very strange had just happened between me and Paul. He knew it and I knew it.

"I've, uh, got to be at Katie's in a few minutes," he added. "She's helping me with my speech. For the historian job."

Katie. So maybe I was wrong. I was definitely wrong.

Katie was helping Paul with his campaign? Ah— that was why he had such professional posters. Katie was really great at art. I guess I should have figured he'd ask her for help. But still . . . was there any part of my life this girl *wasn't* taking over?

"Well, thanks for all the stuff." I stood up.

"And Katie told me to tell you she's really psyched about you interviewing her for the Valentine's Day issue. She said tomorrow morning before first period would be great for her. If you're even back in school."

The last thing I wanted to do was interview Katie. "Um, yeah, sounds good. I'm sure I'll be fine when I wake up."

"Okay, so feel better." He walked toward the

front door, his expression clearly strained.

I opened the door for him, not wanting him to leave, not wanting him to stay. What *did* I want?

He leaned over and kissed me on the cheek. Like he'd done a thousand times before.

But this time I was aware of the feeling. Of his nearness. Of his scent of his soap. He jogged down the steps, turning back to wave, and I smiled at him.

Please let this be the DayQuil affecting my brain and nervous system and heart, I prayed. It *had* to be the cold medicine. It just had to be.

Erica: So, what do you see as the purpose of Valentine's Day?

Katie: [Giggles] Well, isn't that kind of obvious? [More giggles] I can't wait to see Paul all dressed up for the dance. I know he'll look great. I think he should wear a tie, though, but he said he—

Erica: Doesn't like ties, I know. Um, so do you have certain expectations of the holiday?

Katie: Definitely! How could you really like someone and *not* have expectations? It's the one day set aside for mushy, gushy, romantic stuff. Candy, flowers, hearts, you know. And lots and lots of kissing. Did I mention that Paul is the greatest kisser I've ever—

Erica: Okay, Katie, thanks a lot. That's all I need.

Nine

"YOU MADE IT," Paul greeted me as I sat down next to him in history class.

"I feel a lot better," I said brightly. *Well, health-wise.* I smiled at him and he smiled back. *See? Everything's back to normal,* I reassured myself, noticing he was wearing the dark blue sweater I'd given him for Christmas. Noticing how well he filled it out . . .

That's not back to normal, Erica. And you slept off any effects of yesterday's DayQuil.

"There's something I need to talk to you about," he whispered. "It's about Saturday."

"Saturday?"

"Yeah, um, the comic book convention . . ." His eyes darted around the room, looking everywhere but at me. "Well, it *is* on Valentine's Day, and I just—I think I should really be with Katie that day. It's important to her. But you probably know that since you interviewed her, right?"

I stared down at my red notebook.

"That's okay, isn't it?" he asked, concern in his dark eyes. "I mean, you probably want to spend the day with Frank anyway, right?"

A stinging sensation hit the back of my eyelids. Tears.

I willed them away and turned to face him. "That's fine, really. I'm sure Frank will want to do something romantic during the afternoon, so yeah, it's probably better that we cancel."

Actually, Frank hadn't said anything about Saturday afternoon. "You know, maybe I'll just go to the convention with Frank," I told him. "It'll be cool to show him stuff I'm into."

"So this is, like, the first comics convention we've missed—ever," he responded, looking me in the eye. "It'll feel a little weird not to go." I nodded, not knowing what to say. "Oh, and I forgot to tell you yesterday," he continued. "Katie told me about your talk at the Bowl-a-Rama and how much better you made her feel. She'd been worried you were, like, my other girlfriend or something, but after talking to you, she realized how lucky I am to have you for a friend."

His other girlfriend. Other. How dare Katie think I'd ever be just an "other" to Paul!

Whoa! Calm down, Erica. Whatever's going on with you is getting really weird.

"I really need a favor," he whispered. "Tomorrow after school I need to get Katie a Valentine's Day present. Could you help me pick something out?"

What was that stabbing sensation in my chest? I swallowed, grateful that our teacher had just walked in. "No prob," I assured him, realizing that the sensation was my heart twisting.

"So let me get this straight," Linda said, pushing her hair behind her shoulders. "Now you're *upset* about Paul and his new girlfriend? Even with Frank London, Mr. God of journalism, drooling all over you?"

I paused, taking a deep breath. "I'm happy about Paul and Katie, really," I argued. "It's just that for some reason it keeps bugging me that she's, like, taking over everything that used to be mine, you know?"

That was what it was, I'd decided during history class. It wasn't that I was suddenly having feelings for Paul after nine years. It wasn't that I was jealous of him and Katie. And it definitely wasn't that I was really hurt he'd blown me off to spend Valentine's Day with her. I was crazy about Frank.

Linda raised an eyebrow. "Meaning taking over *Paul.*"

"No," I said, staring down at the books in my arms. "I don't want to be Paul's *girlfriend*. I never have, you know that."

"And things are still great with Frank, right?" Linda interrupted, finger-combing her hair as she looked at the mirror on the inside of her locker.

"Yeah." I shifted the books in my arms. "He's . . .

amazing. I just can't help feeling like I'm losing Paul or something, though."

Linda waved her hand in the air dismissively. "Listen, here's the deal. You're used to being Paul's favorite person, and you're just feeling bummed because you're not anymore, and it's kind of a kick in the ego, right?"

I winced. Her harsh words made me feel like such an evil person, especially because I knew they were probably true. "*But,*" she continued, "you'll get over it fast. Especially with someone as gorgeous as Frank London around to ease the blow."

She grinned, and I couldn't help but smile back. Sometimes it was nice to have a friend who was so blunt.

The bell blared. "Thanks, Linda."

Linda's always good for a reality check, I told myself as I strode down the hallway. *I'm probably just weirding out over how Paul is so great at romantic stuff—bringing me soup and tissues when I'm sick, obsessing over a Valentine's Day present, buying me my favorite writer's essays as a congratulatory present for being named one of the commentary editors.* I probably just wished Frank were a little more like that. A little more like Paul. It wasn't that I wanted Paul myself.

That *couldn't* be the case. And after a great afternoon at the comics convention with Frank, and then the most amazing night at the dance, I'd know that for sure. Everything would definitely go back to normal then.

★　　　★　　　★

110

I set down my lunch tray way in the back of the cafeteria, a prime location for researching couples and their behavior. I was sure to get a lot of interesting tidbits, and I *had* to start writing my article for the *Postscript*. I picked up my cheeseburger and looked around the large, crowded room.

My gaze landed on Marie Ikrath, whom I *should* have interviewed. She sat next to her boyfriend, Clinton Arrowood. They were deep in conversation, laughing, talking, laughing, touching, kissing. Marie and Clinton had been together for a long time. I remembered how last Valentine's Day, he'd brought a dozen roses to school and given them to her in front of everyone in the hallway. I'd thought that was so forced, like they had to let *everyone* know how in love they were or something. But now I would probably die from happiness if Frank did something like that.

Clinton picked up Marie's soda and held it out to her so all she had to do was sip. Then he set it back down and kissed her on the cheek. It reminded me of the way Paul could always tell when I wanted something, almost before I knew I did. They held hands, and every now and then Clinton would pull their hands to his lips to kiss hers.

If you felt that way about someone, you wouldn't think PDAs were so gross. Paul's words from that fateful day at the Bowl-a-Rama came back to haunt me. I didn't think what Marie and Clinton were doing was gross at all. I thought it was sweet, beautiful, wonderful. It was *love*. And it was something you couldn't even help doing if you felt that way. You just *wanted* to do it.

I turned away, suddenly feeling as though I was intruding on a private moment.

So now I knew why I hadn't been interviewing people. Hadn't been working on the article. How could I make fun of something that I now took so seriously? That I now understood? PDAs were genuine stuff.

Affection wasn't something to mock.

"Hey, Erica. Observing all the sickening couples, huh?" Frank sat down across from me and unwrapped a sandwich. He'd obviously looked around for me till he found me way back here. That was romantic. Just because he wasn't into PDAs didn't mean he didn't feel what I did.

But what do I feel anymore?

"So, did you get that article done on the school's music program?" he asked, taking a sip of his Coke.

"Oh, wow, I forgot all about it," I admitted, surprised that I had. "I was really sick yesterday, and today I had a lot to get caught up on, and—"

"No problem," he said. "If you could get it done by tomorrow, though . . ."

"Sure," I replied, smiling at him. I realized I was waiting for him to ask me if I felt better, if I needed anything. But he didn't. He probably just had a lot on his mind, between the *Postscript* and his campaign for school historian.

"So I overheard the saddest story while I was waiting on line for my cheeseburger," I told him, squeezing a dollop of ketchup on my fries. "Want some?" I asked.

"Thanks, but I really try to stay away from greasy stuff like that," he reminded me. During that awful double date with Paul and Katie he'd mentioned he didn't eat fries or anything soaked in oil. I guess it hadn't really registered then. How could anyone *not* love fries?

"So what was the tearjerker story you heard?" He rolled his eyes. "I'm sure it'll make me too sick to finish this." He put down his sandwich.

"No, it was actually poignant," I told him, feeling my eyes sparkling. "This guy was telling his girlfriend that when he was in middle school, they had this secret-Santa type of thing for the week of Valentine's Day." Frank nodded, not looking too interested. "And you were supposed to leave stuff in the person's locker every day of the week. So Anthony—"

Frank narrowed his eyes. "It's important to protect the source's confidentiality," he interrupted. "Even if you're just telling *me*."

I swallowed. "I know."

"Hey, don't beat yourself up," he said, smiling. "Just remember it for the future."

That was a little obnoxious, I thought, taking a bite of cheeseburger to hide the expression on my face. Did he ever drop the professional thing? It *was* just me and him; it wasn't as if I'd ever mention names in the article.

Erica, this is what attracted you to Frank in the

first place. He's a serious journalist, for God's sake. Just like you. Chill out.

"Then what?" he prompted.

"So the *source* kept going to his locker every day, all excited about what he'd find. But there was never anything there. And then—this is the worst part—on the last day, he figured there'd be something *really* big there to, you know, make up for the whole week. He got himself all psyched up again, and—"

"There was nothing there," Frank finished, nodding knowingly.

"Yeah," I said. "Isn't that awful?"

"It's exactly why the whole holiday is a giant joke," Frank pronounced.

I frowned, surprised that Frank wasn't affected by the story the way I'd been. Couldn't he picture the look on poor little Anthony's face when he'd opened that empty locker on Friday?

"Oh, and about my interview," Frank added. "Maybe we can do it at the dance. I'm really busy till then because of my campaign for school historian."

I nodded, that last bite of cheeseburger a lump in my stomach. So Frank's own perspective hadn't changed? I'd really thought his feelings for me would make that happen. But he sounded as cynical as he had in the beginning. Did that mean he didn't like me after all?

"Oh, and I was thinking we should get together in the afternoon on Saturday," Frank said, "so we can decide what we'll cover at the dance."

A burst of excitement exploded in me. Frank wanted to spend all of Valentine's Day with me! And he was asking in that same adorable way. Just because *I'd* turned into a mush ball didn't mean Frank had to. And just because *he* wasn't a saphead didn't mean he wasn't crazy about me. Paul's way wasn't the only way. People expressed their feelings differently, that was all.

That was it! That was the slant for my article. All this time I hadn't been able to figure out how to approach it now that I understood PDAs . . . now that *I* had expectations for Valentine's Day.

What a relief! I was so inspired now—and it was all thanks to Frank.

"That sounds great!" I told him. "In fact, there's somewhere I really, really want to go Saturday afternoon and I was hoping you'd go with me. It's a comic book convention that I go to every year. It's so much fun!"

Frank regarded me with a puzzled expression. "A *comic* book convention?" he echoed. "You're kidding."

Had he noticed my face fall? "Uh, no. It really is fun." *Okay, so maybe Frank and I don't agree on absolutely everything. But that's healthier anyway, right?* "But if you're not into it at all, then—"

"I'll go," Frank said. "Though I have to admit I'm a little surprised that someone like *you* would want to spend an afternoon looking at cartoons." He chuckled.

"Comics," I muttered softly, biting my lip.

"What?" he asked.

I shook my head and smiled at him.

"Well, if it's important to you, then of course I'll go." He looked me in the eye, scooting closer. "Erica, I really value this—this *connection* that we have. You know that, right?"

I looked into those sincere, intelligent green eyes. "Yeah," I said shyly. "And hey, it *is* Valentine's Day *all* day."

Frank smiled. "And no self-respecting high-school couple misses a chance to make a big deal out of that," he joked, his eyes twinkling.

High-school couple. My heart started doing ballet moves in my chest. Frank had called us a couple without even blinking.

That was definitely a label.

Erica: So I still don't get why you insisted I interview you. I would have thought you'd run screaming from this tape recorder. Plus, aren't you preoccupied with what to buy Katie for Valentine's Day?

Paul: What are friends for, right? This is to help you with your article. Ooh—we should check out that store.

Erica: Wow, look at all that stuff in the windows! I've never seen so many heart-shaped chocolate boxes and stuffed animals in my life. Hey, but so now you're into sharing your deepest thoughts, even anonymously, with the whole school?

Paul: To help you out, sure, Ms. Commentary Editor.

Erica: Um, okay, so do you have any special Valentine's Day memories?

Paul: Come on, you know everything that's ever happened to me.

Erica: Do you grasp the concept of an interview? [Deep breath] Okay, new question. What do you see as the purpose of Valentine's Day?

Paul: That's easy. It's a day to let your emotions take over, and make someone in your life feel special.

Erica: By giving that person overpriced candy and flowers?

Paul: No, by sharing traditional symbols of love as a way of representing your feelings.

Erica: Is Hallmark paying you off? Hey, stop, no hitting your interviewer. [Scuffling noises] So, wait, you're saying that those little heart-shaped boxes of chocolates are special *because* of the fact that they're *not* unique?

Paul: Hey, no kicking the interviewee! [More scuffling noises] Yeah, that's exactly what I'm saying. Think of it like this—when a guy proposes marriage, he always gives the woman a diamond ring, right? It's a universal thing, not unique in the least. But it's the very meaning behind that old, overdone gesture that makes those diamond rings a big deal.

Erica: [Silence]

Paul: No snappy comeback? You probably think that's the stupidest thing you ever heard, right? Sappy and sentimental.

Erica: [Noisily flips pages in notebook] I'm interviewing *you*, Garabo. Next question. How do you, uh, plan to celebrate Valentine's Day this year?

Paul: With the girl I—well, with Katie.

Erica: [Silent for a long time, then snaps notebook shut] Okay, so thanks, Paul.

Paul: But I thought you had more—

Erica: Nope—I have everything I need. Let's just get this shopping done, okay?

Ten

"THE TEDDY BEAR or the little red devil?" Paul held up the two stuffed animals in front of him.

I groaned. The teddy bear was really adorable. "I don't know, Paul. I don't know her too well."

His smile faded. "The teddy bear is definitely more romantic." He tossed the devil back on the shelf. "Why am I even asking you about stuffed animals? You hate these things."

I used to. I'd probably melt if Frank gave me a cute little teddy bear.

"This is torture for you, huh?" he asked, grinning. "Your biggest nightmare—shopping for Valentine's Day presents."

So he thought that was why I was so cranky. At least he didn't realize it was really because I was getting tired of searching the mall for the absolutely *perfect* gifts for Katie.

"He's got cuter eyes than the devil," I pointed out, handing the bear to Paul.

"You think so?" Paul studied its face very seriously.

I nodded. "Are you ready?" I stumbled as some woman knocked into me on her way to the card section. The place was a war zone that day.

Paul glared at my assailant. "Are you okay?" he asked, turning back to me with concern in his eyes. He put his hand on my shoulder, and once again I was aware of his touch, the weight of his hand, even through my jacket. Tingles danced up my spine and settled at the nape of my neck.

I gulped. *What* was with me? These kinds of feelings were supposed to be reserved for Frank. *His* touch was supposed to do this to me, not *Paul's*.

It's just like Linda said, I told myself. *Some kind of twisted ego thing now that I can't have him. Now that I don't come first. Now that he's in love with someone else.* It was the only explanation that made any sense.

"I'm fine," I reassured him. "It's just so crowded—maybe we should get going now that you have everything."

He nodded, staring at the teddy bear again he'd put in his shopping basket and peeking into the bag in his other hand. We headed to the back of the long line at the cashier. "So I've got the candy and the stuffed animal and the wrapping paper and bows," Paul said.

"And the card you spent a half hour picking out,"

I reminded him. "I think you're done." I stared straight ahead at the rows of helium balloons with sappy messages. Be Mine. Yours Forever. I Love You. Two weeks earlier I would have snapped a picture and wrote a scathing caption about how ridiculous it was to hear those sacred words from a balloon. Now I *wanted* balloons. I wanted everything in that store!

"Don't you think I should get her something a little, like, *personal* too?" Paul asked.

No, I don't. You've only been going out with her for a week and a half. It's not like she deserves the personal kind of presents you always give me.

"Well, maybe something little," I agreed, realizing he was serious about this, actually deeply contemplating it. "If you think you should."

He must really like Katie a lot. Maybe he's even in love.

He stared at me for a second, then pulled me closer to him as a group of women barged past toward the big red-pink-and-white display crammed with candy. "I'm sorry I'm being such a jerk." We inched forward as the line moved ahead.

Paul smirked. "So I guess you and Frank aren't exchanging presents."

"Well, he's just not into that kind of thing," I snapped. *Defensive, defensive.* "People express their feelings differently, Paul." That was my new line, my new official statement on the subject of Valentine's Day. So why did it sound so false?

He shrugged. "Then help me think of what else to get Katie."

We finally reached the cashier, and a few minutes later I was sighing with relief to be out of that store.

"Why don't we just walk around and see if anything catches our eye?" I suggested as we weaved our way through the throngs of people. "What does she like? That would help."

"She's a really good artist," he said. "She loves to draw—maybe I should get her some art supplies. This is so hard," he added. "I never have any trouble buying anything for you." We came upon the huge wishing well in the center of the mall, and Paul plucked a coin from his pocket and tossed it in.

We stared at all the pennies in the bottom of the well. "What did you wish for?" I asked softly.

"Can't tell, silly," he said. "Or it won't come true."

I was sure it had something to do with Katie.

"Here," he said, handing me a penny. "Make a wish."

I took the coin, which felt really warm in my hand, and closed my eyes. *I wish—*

What do *I wish?*

"Oh, I forgot," he said. "Making wishes really isn't your style."

Why did that hurt? It never had been my style, and Paul did know that. So why had he suggested it in the first place?

"I'm keeping the penny," I joked, dropping it in my knapsack.

"Katie and I are getting so close," Paul said, sitting down on a bench in front of the well. "We're pretty much a couple now. It all happened so fast, you know."

I sat down next to him, my chest feeling tight. "Uh-huh. That's great, Paul."

"I wish I knew what else to get her," he continued.

"So *that's* what you wished for," I kidded, gesturing behind us. "I guess it's so easy for us to buy each other presents because we know each other so well. And we love the same things."

He looked at me, then down at the floor. "You know, there was a song playing at the place Katie and I ate at on our first date, and she loved it. I could get her that CD."

I was staring down at the floor too.

"Bad idea?" Paul asked me anxiously.

"No, it's perfect," I almost whispered. "It's sweet."

Paul grinned, then jumped up and grabbed his packages. "Come on. Let's get to the music store, then."

I stood up too and stuck my hands in my pocket. I could feel the penny, still warm from Paul's hand.

Twenty minutes later Paul had another bag and a relieved expression. "Want to stop at Book Nook?" He gestured at my favorite bookstore.

I smiled. Paul knew that I never came to the mall without spending a long time drooling over all the books I wanted in there. We walked inside, and I checked out the new releases first, then we headed in the direction of the writing and journalism section in the back.

I stopped dead in my tracks. Frank was standing in the aisle, his back to us; he was holding the book I'd told him I was dying to get. I whirled around and grabbed Paul, yanking him behind the nearest display.

"What are you doing?" he yelped.

"Shh," I whispered, putting my finger to my lips. We huddled behind the display, our shoulders pressed together. Yet again I was very aware of him, very aware of his hand on my back. I glanced at him, and his cheeks were flushed, his eyes even darker than usual. He was looking at me with that same expression he'd had the day he told me he had *those* feelings for me.

But that definitely wasn't the case now. He was clearly into Katie. All he felt for me at that moment was concern. After all, only a psycho would have grabbed him and thrown him behind the display without an explanation.

"It's Frank," I whispered, peeking around the books. He wasn't standing in the aisle any longer. I shuffled to the other side of the display and poked my head out. Frank was at the register, buying the book.

I watched him leave the store, then stood up, my legs feeling rubbery from kneeling. Paul stood up too, eyeing me as though I were crazy.

"What was *that* all about?" he asked.

"I-It's stupid, really," I stammered. "I saw Frank back there, and I figured he was getting something for me for Valentine's Day. I didn't want him to see me and ruin the surprise." Suddenly that barely seemed relevant—I was still trying to get my heart rate under control and my hands to stop trembling.

Being so close to Paul just then had done

something very un-best-friend-like to me. My neck wasn't used to getting goose bumps just because it was so near Paul's lips.

Paul shook his head. "Since when do you stoop to such crazy behavior for a *guy?*"

"What?" I asked, gulping. *Wait—he means Frank,* I realized with relief. "Okay, it was silly," I admitted, tracing the cover of a book in the sale bin next to me. My fingers were still shaking slightly, but my pulse was slowly returning to normal. "But I was just surprised to see him buying me a present, that's all." I'd told him how badly I wanted that book and how I couldn't afford it because it's in hardcover.

"He is your boyfriend, though." Paul slapped himself on the forehead. A little lock of dark hair fell across his brow. "Oops, I forgot. You guys don't believe in buying presents, or in anything romantic."

"Don't be so sure about that," I said huffily. "Yesterday he even called us a couple." I stood straighter. "He's got a romantic side too . . . he just doesn't like to show it that much."

"A romantic side?" Paul laughed, his straight white teeth gleaming. "Doesn't that go against everything in your little article?"

I flinched. "I'm not—it isn't—" I sighed. "Forget it, okay?" I turned away, embarrassed by the tears welling up in my eyes. "Can we just go home?"

"Erica, I didn't mean to—"

I glared at him, and he shut up. We walked out of the bookstore in strained silence.

Linda had been wrong. This thing with Paul had

nothing to do with jealousy or my ego. It was much more than that. I had changed. Everything was different. How I felt about dating, romance, stuffed animals, Hallmark cards, and . . . Paul?

Is it valid to put a price on the value of being in a school band? What about trying to compare the value of that experience with, say, playing on the field hockey team?

I stared at the words, watching as they all blurred together on the page, then crumpled up the paper and tossed it onto the floor, where the remains of my last twenty attempts lay in a heap. Ever since Frank had referred to us as a couple I couldn't seem to write one sentence of an article without freaking out over what he'd think of it.

I pulled a fresh sheet of paper out of my notebook and tried again, making an effort to capture Frank's style as I wrote. But it sounded so forced, so not *me*.

This is hopeless, I thought in frustration, staring off into space.

"Honey? You okay?"

I glanced up at the doorway of my bedroom. My mom was watching me with a frown.

"I'm fine." I flashed her a brief smile. "There's just . . . stuff going on right now."

"What kind of stuff?" she asked, sitting next to me on the bed.

"I don't know," I moaned. "Things with Frank are really great, but I'm not sure we have that much in common."

"Like you and Paul do, you mean." She smiled at me. Why did moms always know so much? I'd barely told her anything about Frank, just that we were dating and I really liked him.

I nodded. "It's weird, but I've always been able to talk to Paul about writing and reporting too, even though that's not the big thing in his life. And as much as I like being with Frank, it's not comfortable the way it is with Paul. Frank and I don't really have *fun* together, you know?"

"Well, honey," she said gently, "Frank *isn't* Paul. Things *are* going to be different with him. But didn't you also say you hadn't shown him many of the things you enjoy? Like comics and bowling and skee ball and a mountain of french fries? Maybe you'd have fun together if you did the things you liked."

She was right.

I stay away from greasy stuff like that . . .

Okay, so he didn't like french fries. But once he saw all the cool comics at the convention, he'd definitely understand why they were great. He might even become a huge fan, and then he and Paul would have more in common too. And what guy didn't like skee ball or bowling?

Frank isn't Paul . . .

Garfield meowed. "There's my cue," my mom said, getting up. "Come talk later if you need to."

"Thanks, Mom," I called out as she left, jumping up to grab the phone. It was Katie, of all people.

"I was wondering if you could give me some

127

advice," she said, "about what to get Paul for Valentine's Day."

I sucked in my breath. Was this some kind of test? Because I was quickly approaching my limit. Frank and I might not have that much in common outside journalism, but even I didn't need to consult anyone on what to get him for Valentine's Day. I was planning on getting him a leather-bound journal and a funky pen.

"Well," I said slowly, sitting at my desk, "what were you thinking of?"

"I don't know," Katie confessed. "That's why I figured I should call you. I mean, since you know him better than anyone."

Each of her words was like a dart thrown at me carelessly, with that last sentence hitting the bull's-eye dead on.

Better than anyone . . . was that even true anymore?

"You know he likes bowling," I said. I drummed my fingers on my desk. "And video games. And . . . comic books."

"Uh-huh." She paused. "Unfortunately. Could you tell how much I hated every minute at the Bowl-a-Rama?"

Huh? "I knew you weren't thrilled," I said. "But you *hated* it?"

"Please don't tell Paul—I know he'd be hurt, but I'm just not into that stuff."

"Okay, so you're not gonna get him his own pair of tacky bowling shoes."

Katie laughed. "No way."

"Then what about a video? Paul loves wacky comedies." I smiled, remembering the way he could always crack me up imitating Monty Python.

"I know," Katie said. "He does have a great sense of humor, even with all those corny jokes he's always telling."

Corny jokes? That was one of the best things about Paul! What did Katie see in him if she couldn't appreciate how fun he was?

"I'm not sure what else to suggest," I said.

"It probably sounds like I'm totally ragging on Paul," she said. "But I really like him a lot. He's . . . he's so sweet."

Yeah, sweet, and funny, and zany, and adventurous, and tons of other things Katie just didn't appreciate.

Stop it, I scolded myself. *If Katie and Paul are happy together, it's not my place to think for either of them.*

"I have an idea," I told her. "Why don't you draw something for him? Paul mentioned that you're a pretty good artist."

"Really? He did?"

"Yep." I dug my toes into the carpet. "I know he'd like it if you drew a picture, you know, just for him." I could imagine the way Paul would light up when he saw it, how his eyes would crinkle at the corners from the huge smile that would spread across his face.

I gulped. *I'm doing the right thing,* I told

myself, twisting my hands together in my lap.

"Thanks, Erica, that's a great idea."

"No problem." I took a deep breath.

"Okay—bye, and thanks again."

"Uh-huh. Bye." I dropped the receiver down with a satisfying thud, and immediately covered my face with my hands.

Eleven

"THAT'S IT FOR the sports section," Mr. Serson said as Jolie sat down. "Commentary editors?" Frank stood, and I started to join him, but he put his hand on my shoulder.

"I'll cover it," he said. I stared up at him. We were *co*editors. That meant we gave our article announcements to the staff *together*. He smiled and winked at me, then squeezed around everyone as he strode to the front of the room.

"What was *that* about?" Linda whispered.

I shrugged. Frank cleared his throat. "After the upcoming Valentine's Day issue," he began, disgust dripping from his voice, "we're finally going to focus on something *important*: the topic of violence and safety in high schools. The commentary section will be devoted to it."

What?

"Carrie, I know you're production, but we

could use the extra help in research. If you could collect points of view on the locker search question, and . . ."

I tuned him out as he continued making the assignments, my mouth hanging open in shock. I hadn't heard *anything* about this. My hands clenched into fists and my whole body tightened up in anger.

Linda nudged me hard in the rib cage. "What's the matter?" she whispered.

"I'll tell you later," I murmured. I didn't want to make a scene in the middle of the meeting.

I listened in shock as Frank ran through all the assistants and explained everything that we wanted for the commentary section. By the time he wrapped it up and sat back down next to me, my blood was boiling.

I started tapping the floor with my foot and folded my arms across my chest, gripping my upper arms with my hands. My nails dug into my skin through the thin turtleneck I had on.

"Okay," Mr. Serson finally announced. "That's it for today. And I promise—no more staff meetings during lunch period." Everyone got up. "Erica, Frank—stay for a minute, please."

"I'll call you later," Linda whispered.

"How come you were flying solo up there?" Mr. Serson asked Frank when everyone else had cleared out. My ears perked up, waiting for the explanation.

"Oh, Erica didn't know about this stuff," Frank

said. "The other editors and I came up with it on Monday—Erica was out sick."

You could have told me about it, I thought angrily. *Like during any of the days between Monday and today.*

Why couldn't I say that out loud? I'd never had a problem flipping out on Paul when he did something that ticked me off.

"I kind of wish you *had* told me, actually," I said.

"I'm sorry," Frank began, "but you were sick, and I knew you had a lot to catch up on with schoolwork and that article you wrote about the school band, which, by the way, was excellent."

Excellent? So he'd liked my final version? I was relieved, since I'd had such a hard time with it, but it was weird that he thought it was excellent when I thought it was so dull.

"I assumed I was doing you a favor by working this other stuff out on my own," Frank explained, his tone completely sincere.

I glanced up at Mr. Serson, who was nodding slowly. "You had the right intentions," he assured Frank. "But in the future, you guys should do everything together. That's why there are two of you, okay?"

Frank nodded. "Of course. Sorry, Erica."

I smiled weakly. Frank shuffled some papers, and when Mr. Serson left, he reached for my hand. "I really didn't know you'd take it this way," he said.

I gazed down at the floor, tracing the linoleum square with my sneaker.

133

"Erica?" he asked softly, reaching out to put his hands on my arms.

I looked up at him, searching his face for the truth. His green eyes were serious, and I felt my anger start to drain.

I bit my lip. We didn't need to get in some big argument right before Valentine's Day. "I'm glad you liked my article on the band."

"It was *brilliant*," he responded. He stepped closer to me and cupped my chin in his palm.

I backed up a step, and his hand dropped. *That's weird of me,* I thought. I was a little upset, though, so I guess it made sense that I wasn't in the mood for him to kiss me or something.

"Are you really that mad at me?" Frank asked.

"I'll get over it," I said, smiling. "Look, let's just forget it, okay?"

"Okay," he agreed. "Good. Because I have to get something done here and I won't be able to hang the rest of the posters you made, so I thought you wouldn't mind . . ."

My eyebrows shot up. He was choosing that particular moment to request favors?

"I'm sorry to ask," he said. "But I've got a test to study for, and tomorrow morning is the debate, so I want to go over my speech one more time. You did such a great job on the posters, so I'm really psyched to get them all up."

I sighed, rubbing my temples as my head started to throb.

"Where are they?" I asked, smiling thinly.

Frank reached under the desk and pulled out a bag. "Thank you so much, Erica. You're a life-saver."

I smiled. "Good luck with your work. I'll stop by to let you know when I'm done."

"Okay, great. See you later." He sat down and clicked on the laptop.

Dismissed.

Shouldn't he be groveling for my forgiveness? Trying to kiss me as affectionate thanks for agreeing to miss lunch while I put up his posters?

Whatever. Maybe some quiet time alone with the walls of Emerson High would help me figure things out.

There. Done. I finally got the last poster taped up straight. I stepped back, nodding appreciatively at my work. So maybe I wasn't the best artist in the world, but at least the perfectionist in me wouldn't hang something up the slightest bit crookedly.

I grabbed my supplies, then headed toward the cafeteria. I was starving!

The second I turned the corner I heard giggling. I had a feeling I was about to interrupt a make-out session. Just two weeks earlier that would have made me lose my appetite. Now it just made me wistful.

I glanced at the couple—and froze.

Paul and Katie.

Paul and Katie . . . kissing.

I gulped, and my arms went limp. The bag of

tape fell onto the floor with a loud crash. At least, it sounded pretty loud in the silence that suddenly filled the hall. Paul and Katie jumped apart and stared at me.

"I-I'm—I'm sorry," I stammered, watching as the tape started to roll across the floor toward them. My body wasn't responding to the commands my brain was sending it. *Mouth, stop gaping. Arms, reach down and pick up your stuff.* And the most important part that wasn't working: *Legs, get moving, now.*

Only my eyes were functioning—and way too well. They couldn't stop staring at Paul and Katie's hands, still linked together.

They'd been hanging posters too, I realized, noting the two lying on the floor by Katie's feet. The paralysis lifted, and I chased down my tape.

"Hi," Katie said, her face bright red. I wondered if mine matched. "We were hanging up some final posters."

"Yeah, me too." I avoided looking at Paul.

"So where's Frank?" he asked.

"He has some important newspaper work," I told him, "so I offered to finish hanging his posters for him." It was amazing how much easier it was to lie when you didn't meet the person's gaze.

"That's nice of you," Katie chimed in.

I glanced up at Katie's poster, awed by how great it looked. The colors all worked together perfectly, and your eyes were drawn right to the important elements, the reasons why Paul would make a good school historian.

Katie glanced at me, then at Paul. "So, uh, maybe we should get going."

Paul's cheeks turned bright red. "Yeah, we'd better go," he said, clearing his throat. "We'll see you later, Erica." He picked up their stuff, then put his arm around Katie and hustled her down the hall. They disappeared into the cafeteria, and the big orange doors swung shut behind them.

I sank down onto the floor, rolling the tape around in my hands.

What's wrong with me? I wondered, pulling my knees up to my chest. Why had seeing them kiss totally stopped my brain from operating my body?

I practically ran back to the *Postscript* office, anxious to let Frank know his posters were up so I could go veg out in the library with my sandwich and chill out before my next class. I was about to walk into the room when I heard Paul's voice, his *angry* voice, coming from inside the room.

"You're taking advantage of her, and I think that sucks!"

What is he talking about? And who's he talking to? I huddled closer to the half-open door, making sure I was hidden from view.

"I shouldn't have let it go on this long," Paul continued, "but I kept hoping Erica would figure things out for herself." I couldn't believe what I was hearing. How *dare* Paul go behind my back and interfere in my life like this!

"You're just upset because you have no chance at school historian," Frank retorted.

"This is about *Erica*," Paul snapped.

I shook my head in disbelief, furious. Even though he had Katie, Paul *still* thought he could jump in and try to keep a guy away from me! Whom I dated was *my* decision to make, not Paul's.

"You asked Erica out right before the election was officially announced," Paul said, his tone ice cold. "*Very* interesting timing to develop an interest in such a great writer. Especially one who happened to be friends with your *competition*. You *knew* I was thinking of running for historian—I'd mentioned it a few times at yearbook meetings."

Omigod. Paul thought Frank was *using* me? Was that what my supposed best friend thought of me?

I refused to listen to another word. I burst inside. "Well, well," I said through clenched teeth, my eyes fixed on Paul with a glare. "What's going on?"

Frank looked at Paul and raised his eyebrows.

"It's nothing," Paul said tightly.

"Would you mind giving us a minute alone?" I asked Frank.

He shrugged. "No problem. I was done here anyway." He collected his stuff and headed out, stopping to give me a quick kiss good-bye.

"I'm sorry about this," I whispered before Frank pulled away.

He shook his head. "Don't worry about it," he reassured me. "Are the posters all up?"

I nodded, feeling a strange twist in my stomach.

He wants to know about the posters when he just had a huge fight with my best friend?

No, I told myself sternly. *Don't let Paul's jealous accusations get to you.*

"Great. I'll call you later. You can interview me tonight for the Valentine's article—it'll give us a good excuse to talk a long time on the phone." He glared at Paul, then slammed the door shut behind him.

"What were you *thinking?*" I yelled at Paul. "Are you really that immature that you have to have it all? Frank was right." I shook my head. "You're just jealous. Because of the historian campaign *and* because I like him!"

"This is *not* about jealousy," he shouted back. "Yeah, I can't stand the jerk. I've hated him long before I ever knew you liked him, Erica. And there's no doubt in my mind that he's using you. He just wanted to make sure you didn't help me with my campaign. I'd bet anything on it. So excuse me for not wanting to see you get hurt!" He started to brush past me toward the door.

"Wait a minute!" I grabbed his arm. "How dare you! It's so impossible to believe Frank London could actually like me? Thanks a lot, Paul. You *are* jealous! You're just—"

"Just *what?*" he interrupted, his tone like ice. "Just too hung up on you?" He pulled out of my grasp. "I think it's time you got over yourself."

I stumbled back as though I'd been slapped hard across the face. My legs buckled, and I sank into a chair.

Paul had never talked to me like that before. *Never.*

He took a deep breath. "I didn't mean to say that."

I smiled weakly. "Yeah, you did."

"Look, maybe we just need a break, you know?" he said.

I looked at him in bewilderment. "A . . . break?" I asked, my voice cracking.

He nodded. "Time apart."

"Okay," I agreed, though it wasn't okay at all.

"So . . . I'll see you."

And then he was gone.

Erica: I guess I don't have to ask if you have any special memories of Valentine's Day.

Frank: You need to get every side of a story, Erica, so it's still worth asking.

Erica: Okay, then—

Frank: Write that down, for yourself. [Slowly] *Every side of the story.*

Erica: [Scribbles some doodles on page] Got it. So?

Frank: I remember throwing up one day in junior high after eating a box of chocolates some guy gave my older sister.

Erica: [Trying not to laugh] So what do you see as the purpose of the holiday?

Frank: It's clearly a Hallmark-manufactured occasion to generate revenue during a month without any other major holidays.

Erica: But everyone buys into it. Why do you think that is?

Frank: Everyone in our culture is desperate for empty symbols of feeling. They cling to Valentine's Day as a chance to pretend there is real substance to their relationships.

Erica: Some people say that those symbols are simply good ways to express feelings that are sometimes hard to share. So red roses and stuffed teddy bears are kind of like engagement rings. We give them to each other because they're easy to recognize as gifts of love and affection.

141

Frank: [Chortles] Who's been feeding you that line?

Erica: [Swallows hard] I'm just, uh, playing devil's advocate. Taking the other point of view, the other side, to point out there *is* one.

Frank: That's good. It's an important skill to master.

Erica: Okay, so—

Frank: Write that down. [Slowly] *Play devil's advocate.*

Twelve

"AND THAT'S WHY you should cast your votes for me, Frank London!" he finished, stepping back from the podium as the auditorium filled with applause. I clapped my hands together mechanically.

Paul and Katie were sitting in the front row.

I'd arrived late for the assembly, wanting to avoid running into Linda or Sharon; they would have taken one look at my expression and known something was majorly wrong. If I talked about what happened with Paul earlier, I'd burst into tears. And I definitely didn't want to do that. So I'd slipped in late, taking a seat in the last row.

We'd already heard Jamie Waters's speech, Jennifer Connell's, and now Frank's. Frank had been better prepared than Jamie or Jen, and everyone in our class already looked up to him as this supersmart guy, even if he wasn't exactly popular. I'd noticed with pleasure that Frank had taken my advice about toning down the vocabulary in his speech.

"The next and final candidate is Paul Garabo," Mr. Kensington announced. Paul stood, then leaned down while Katie whispered something in his ear. As he jogged up the steps to the stage, my heart constricted in my chest. He hated me now. He'd made that clear.

"I'm probably the last person everyone expected to see up here," Paul began, resting his arms on the podium. "I'm not usually running for big positions or doing much of anything to make myself stand out. In fact, that's actually why being school historian appeals to me so much."

He paused, glancing in Katie's direction. I could imagine the supportive smile she was flashing him. "You see," Paul continued, "I don't *want* to stand out. I want to be a part of a class full of people who all have their own special talents, skills, and abilities. I want to represent us as a whole. So that's why instead of talking about who I am and what I can do, I'd rather talk about *us,* and who we are as a school."

I listened as he launched into a discussion of all the different accomplishments of our students, and his ideas for the next year's yearbook. I was blown away by how genuine his passion was. Maybe he didn't sound as polished as Frank, but he was so much more *real.*

I sighed, leaning back in my seat and fidgeting with my nails. *I really should want Frank to win,* I told myself. *Frank's my . . . boyfriend. And*

Paul is barely even a friend at this point.

But watching Paul up there, so full of energy and enthusiasm, all I wanted was for him to have everything that would make him happy. I winced, realizing that my friendship no longer seemed to fit in that category.

"Hey, Erica," a voice called out as I headed to math class. I whirled around and saw Sharon running up behind me. "So Paul was pretty awesome, huh?" she asked, watching me closely.

"What?" I stepped over to the side of the hallway so that we weren't in anyone's way.

Sharon rolled her eyes. "His speech this morning?"

"Oh, right." She kept looking at me intently, her large blue eyes narrowing. "Yeah, he was great," I said, shifting my backpack higher on my shoulder. "And so was Frank, wasn't he?" The words came out kind of high-pitched and squeaky, and I knew I was busted.

"Spill it," Sharon ordered.

I sighed, leaning back against the wall. "Paul and I aren't really talking," I confessed, watching Sharon's eyes bug out.

"You're not *what?*" she asked.

"It's . . . it's a long story." I glanced down at my watch. "Class starts in a few minutes."

"I'm aware," she replied. Her gaze softened. "Er, you look totally miserable, and it doesn't seem like Frank even matters much at all."

"No," I jumped in. "That's not . . . he definitely

matters. But it's hard when I'm so mixed up over this Paul stuff, you know? Granted, my knees don't exactly go all Jell-O anymore around Frank," I admitted. "But that's natural, right? It just means we're more comfortable together."

Of course, if that were true, then how come I still felt a twinge of awkwardness when I talked to him, the way I had in the beginning? Why hadn't I told him how upset I still was over the way he'd taken control of the commentary section without telling me? Or how upset I was about the fight he'd had with Paul? Or how totally miserable I was that Paul wasn't talking to me anymore?

Katie was walking down the hall toward us. She glanced up at the exact moment I noticed her. Our eyes met, and she smiled nervously, then came over to us. "Hi, Erica," she said, hugging her books to her chest. "Um, thanks again for your advice. You know, about what to give Paul for Valentine's Day."

Had Paul told her about our fight? I doubted that.

I ignored the surprised expression on Sharon's face. "Oh, no problem," I said. "I'm just glad you guys are so happy." Yeah, glad. I was very glad in that way of being really . . . *not* glad.

I shifted uncomfortably, pondering the best way to make a fast exit. Then I saw Cami, a girl from the student government, approaching with a candygram in her hands. My heart jumped. A candygram! Maybe Paul hadn't meant what he'd said about taking a break. Why else would he still keep up the tradition of sending me a candygram for

Valentine's Day?

A grin spread across my face as I anticipated what kind of supersappy you're-my-best-friend message he'd come up with this year. I had a huge collection of these in my desk drawer at home. *It was crazy to think Paul would really let our friendship end,* I told myself as Cami reached us. I had definitely blown things out of proportion.

"Here," Cami said, holding out the candygram. But she was looking at *Katie*. I froze, the smile dropping off my lips. "To Katie, from Paul," Cami read, handing the candygram to Katie.

Katie's eyes lit up, and she clasped the bag of candy in one hand, then opened up the card. She broke out in a smile when she read the private message. "He's so sweet," she said, glancing up at me.

I managed to nod. "Uh-huh," I choked out. What was wrong with me? Of *course* Paul would be sending candygrams to his girlfriend instead of me, his *former* best friend.

The bell rang; Katie smiled and hurried off to class. Sharon faced me with sympathy practically oozing out of her pores. "Er," she began, "you and Paul aren't talk—"

"I have to go." I rushed down the hallway. I couldn't believe I was being such an idiot. I'd always teased Paul mercilessly about those stupid candygrams, and now I was about to cry because he hadn't sent me one.

That meant he was serious about taking that

break. He didn't want to be my friend anymore.

I stepped into the *Postscript* office, anxious to get to work on my Valentine's Day article and shut out the rest of the world.

Frank sat at his desk. Gorgeous, intelligent, devoted Frank. The sight of him should have cheered me up considerably. But just then it . . . didn't.

"Hey, Erica! I'm glad you're here."

"Really?" I dropped my backpack on the floor and leaned against the edge of his desk.

He nodded. "Uh-huh. I've been thinking how we definitely have to write about the candygrams. Maybe one of those dumb lists of the top ten reasons why candygrams are the stupidest way to express how you feel."

I winced. "Yeah, I guess we could do that." I hated candygrams now.

Frank narrowed his eyes. "Is something wrong?" he asked.

I shrugged. "It's sort of a long story. But I actually came here to work on that article, so I guess it is good we're both here." I paused, taking a deep breath. "Why don't we start with the candygrams? What should we say?"

"We can point out that for two dollars you get this tiny bag of candy," he suggested.

I cracked a smile. I had always made that same point to Paul. Of course, that was before I'd been devastated that I was no longer worth a two-dollar bag of M&Ms.

So that's the point, I realized. *Worth.* Special tokens of affection were all about showing people how much they meant to you. Whether it was a two-dollar bag of candy or a gazillion-dollar necklace or something you made from scratch that didn't cost a penny, it was all about making the other person feel cherished.

I sat forward in my chair. "Don't forget to mention the girls who spend the end of the day crying in the bathroom because they didn't get one."

Frank rolled his eyes. "Are you serious?" he asked.

I gulped. "Yeah," I said. "It's the truth." *Especially when your own best friend doesn't send you one because he—* Why *weren't* Paul and I talking? It had made sense when he told me he wanted the break, because of the fight and the tension, but now it seemed so complicated.

Was it because we just weren't getting along? Because of Frank? Because of Katie? Because he'd moved on and was now in love with someone else?

Or was it because he really thought Frank was using me and because I'd yelled at him, accusing him of jealousy?

You're the one who's jealous. You're upset that Paul doesn't feel that way about you anymore just when you started to very bizarrely feel that way about him. When you've learned that everything you thought you wanted isn't what you want at all.

You want candygrams from the guy you have every reason to love. The guy you have fun with. The guy who brings you tissues and soup when you're sick, collects your homework assignments, tells off your boyfriend when he's sure you're being used. The guy who makes you feel like you're totally, one hundred percent okay.

I felt my eyes watering up. I couldn't cry there, in front of Frank.

"I just remembered I have to be somewhere," I said hastily, grabbing my backpack.

"What?" Frank stared at me, tilting his head in confusion. "But you just got here."

"Yeah, I know. I—I remembered something I have to do at home."

"Okay. I guess I'll see you tomorrow?"

Tomorrow.

Valentine's Day.

Thirteen

"**O**H, LOOK!" I squealed, pointing to a table across the room. "There's a whole corner devoted to Wonder Woman."

Frank wrinkled his nose. "Wonder Woman?" he asked with obvious disgust.

I sighed. Frank's nose had gotten a lot of exercise so far that day. Every time I tried to show him something I liked, he would scrunch up his face as if I were trying to convince him to come pick through garbage with me.

"Is there anything here you *want* to see?" I snapped, totally exasperated.

Frank sighed. "Erica, you knew this wasn't my thing," he said, backing up as someone dressed as Spider-Man squeezed by us. "I'm sorry, but I'm not going to be excited by . . . *comic* books." There went the nose again.

"Then why did you agree to come here?" I asked.

He looked at me in surprise. "For you," he explained, as though it was utterly obvious.

I felt guilty. I *did* know that—I'd been really happy that he was willing to spend a day looking at stuff he hated to make me happy. So why had I expected more of him once we were there? Why was I pressing him to be someone he wasn't? Frank didn't care about vintage Superman books, or comparing the way different artists drew the Joker. Frank wasn't . . .

Paul.

I bit my lip. Why did everything come back to Paul?

"I'm sorry," I said. "You're right, I'm being really unfair." I forced a smile. "Do you want to get out of here?"

His eyes filled with relief. "I'd love to."

"All right," I agreed, disappointed that I'd have to cut out so early. I was failing miserably at my first real Valentine's Day. "Let me just go get—"

"Erica!" I turned and saw the grinning face of Matthew Wilde, another convention regular whom Paul and I had gotten to know over the years. "Where's Paul?" he asked.

I swallowed. "He's, uh, not here," I mumbled. I sensed Frank stiffen next to me. "Frank, this is Matt," I said awkwardly. "Matt, this is my—um, this is Frank."

Matt nodded at Frank. "What do you mean, Paul's not here? He would die over these!" He shifted the pile of comics in his hand, all X-Men, Paul's favorite.

"He's with his girlfriend today," I explained. "She's not into comics."

"Me either," Frank said with a laugh. "Erica? We were just heading out," he added to Matt.

Matt looked at my empty hands. "But you didn't buy anything yet! You always have armfuls—"

"It was great meeting you," Frank interrupted, "but we've really gotta go."

He smiled thinly at Matt, then draped an arm around my shoulder and edged me forward.

"What's the matter?" I asked when he got outside. "Is there a reason you went all Road Runner on me? That was pretty rude, don't you think?"

"It's just frustrating how *seriously* you and your friends seem to take these juvenile things," he explained.

I came to a halt and pulled my jacket tighter around me. "What?"

"Look, I'm sorry," he said. "I shouldn't lump you together with them. I know you're not as immature as the people you hang out with. I just don't understand how you can bear their company, that's all."

I sucked in my breath.

Frank stepped closer to me, brushing a strand of hair away from my face. His fingertips lingered on my cheek. "Let's not talk about this, okay?" he asked gently. "Let's just . . . forget about this whole afternoon, and focus on tonight, and the dance." He stared at me, his lips curling up into a smile. "I think it's going to be a lot of fun for us."

Why couldn't I imagine having fun with Frank anywhere?

At least he's trying again, I told myself. *Telling me he's looking forward to the dance, excited about it. He's not even pretending to use our Postscript section as an excuse anymore. Tonight's going to be special. He has a present for you and everything!*

I knew he'd like the burgundy leather-covered journal and retro rosewood pen I'd bought for him that morning. I'd even picked out a cute Valentine's Day card for him. Nothing mushy, of course. Tasteful and almost masculine and—

"Hey, so I forgot to tell you," Frank said, cutting into my thoughts "I was in the Book Nook the other day and I bought that hardcover you recommended. It's really good. You can borrow it when I'm done. Just don't break the spine—I hate that, don't you?"

My blood actually stopped flowing.

I was the biggest idiot in the world.

I forced myself to nod. We continued walking to the bus stop, though I couldn't believe my legs were working.

Maybe his going to the dance with me really *was* just about the *Postscript*. Maybe he *hadn't* been making a cute excuse about going to the dance together as a research mission.

Or maybe he just wasn't the type to give Valentine's Day presents, I reminded myself. *Duh. That doesn't mean he isn't into taking you to the dance in a romantic sense.*

I honestly had no clue now what to expect that night. On one hand, I didn't even know how I felt about Frank anymore. But on the other, I wanted Paul to be wrong about him.

Maybe *I* just didn't want to be wrong about him.

I peered at him out of the corner of my eye. Suddenly the intense expression I'd always found so adorable just looked . . . cold. I couldn't think of any more excuses for the way my feelings for Frank had changed over the past week.

It wasn't because of the weird feelings I'd developed for Paul. It was because *Frank* wasn't right for me. Everything Paul had been saying about him was starting to seem frighteningly true. *Even,* I thought with a sharp pang, *the possibility that Frank has really just been using me all along. To stop me from helping Paul.*

Well, you always wanted his respect for your writing talent, Erica. If he was using you, at least you'll know he really does think you're talented.

Oh, yeah. Like that would really make me feel any better.

"You look amazing," Ellen said, shaking her head. She was sitting cross-legged on my bed, watching as I freaked over getting ready for a dance that I was dreading with every ounce of my being.

"Are you sure this skirt doesn't make my thighs look huge?" I asked her. I wasn't too sure if Frank would even comment on the special care I'd taken with my outfit and hair. But Paul and Katie would be at the dance, and I needed to show them that I was looking and feeling *great*. Well, I needed to show Paul that, at least.

She laughed. "As if that's possible," she replied, pulling her own skinny legs up to her chest. "Go check yourself out."

I stared in the full-length mirror on the back of my bedroom door. Whoa! The black miniskirt made my legs look really long—not huge at all. And the clingy maroon velvet top that Linda had insisted I buy during a mall run was festive and sexy. I had on high heels too. It was the polar opposite of Drab Day attire.

"See? You look awesome!" Ellen exclaimed.

The doorbell rang, and I froze. "That's Frank," I blurted out, a thousand butterflies in my stomach. My feelings for him might have changed, but I was psyched to see what he'd be wearing. He usually dressed nicely, so I figured he'd be really decked out.

"I want details later," Ellen told me, then scampered into our parents' room.

I took a deep breath, snatched up my little beaded evening purse, and headed downstairs. Another deep breath at the front door.

I plastered a smile on my face and swung open the door.

My smile vanished.

Frank wore the exact same clothes he'd had on at the convention—jeans and a long-sleeved green polo shirt.

Frank's face paled a few shades and his eyes opened

wide as he stared at my outfit. I quickly stepped backward, so that the door would block as much of my body as possible. Then his face broke into a wide grin.

"I love it!" he cried.

I stared at him in confusion. Was this his strange way of complimenting how I looked?

"You're going *undercover*," he stated matter-of-factly. "I wish I'd thought of that. It's brilliant! You'll look like all the other silly girls in their little dresses, so you'll have a much easier time eavesdropping on their stupid conversations for our section! Me, though, I'll stand out like a sore thumb. I've been looking forward to this research trip all week, and I hadn't even thought of it!"

"That's right," I said, plastering that fake smile back on my face. "That's me, always thinking about the article." *Does this idiot even recognize sarcasm when he hears it? Or does he just never really listen at all?*

He grinned at me. "And it's so *cute* that you've tried so hard to look sexy!"

You're the biggest jerk I've ever met in my entire life, I told him silently.

At least now I knew for sure. It was funny—I didn't even hate Frank. He'd never hidden the fact that he was a jerk. I just hadn't recognized it. We were going to the dance to do research for our article. It was strictly professional.

The second Paul saw me in this outfit and Frank in his jeans, he'd be able to say *I told you so.*

Maybe it's a good thing he's not talking to me, then.

157

Fourteen

"LOOK AT THIS place!" Frank cried out in disgust as we entered the school gym.

"Yeah, I know," I said wistfully, staring around me. Pink and red streamers were draped all over the walls and strewn across the floor, and balloons floated above us. It looked like the perfect setting to be in with someone you loved, someone you—

"What did they do, buy out a florist?" Frank continued. I glanced at all the tables set up with delicate rose arrangements. So maybe there had been a time when I would have scoffed at that too, but now the decorations and flowers took my breath away. They were beautiful.

"Why don't we go sit down?" I asked, anxious not to be standing in full view at the entrance. Frank was carrying two full-size notebooks—he'd been *thoughtful* enough to bring an extra one for me.

"Let's see, where's the best vantage point?"

Frank asked, scanning the room. "Oh, look, your two friends seem happy."

I followed his gaze and saw Paul and Katie slow-dancing near the stage.

My heart twisted. Paul looked amazing. He wore a long-sleeved button-down gray shirt tucked neatly into a pair of nice black pants. Katie looked as pretty as ever in a red dress.

Tears welled up in my eyes, and I furiously blinked them away. *What would it be like to be in his arms?* I wondered. *To be pressed so close against him? To kiss him . . .*

He hated me now, but I still wanted him to be happy. *I guess that's how you feel when you really— When you really loved someone.*

I forced myself to look away, taking a lungful of air. I spotted Linda snuggled up against Dave, and Sharon dancing closely with her date, a guy her sister had set her up with. Everyone looked so happy, nestled in each other's arms as though that was the safest and most wonderful place to be. How could I ever have thought affection was something to mock?

And why had I thought I could handle coming to the dance? I should have slammed the door in Frank's face and told him to research alone. But I hadn't been able to do it. And it wasn't as if I could leave the dance now. I couldn't bear giving Frank the satisfaction of knowing he'd hurt me. I couldn't bear to have Paul know how miserable I was either.

"How about in that corner over there?" I asked Frank, a shiver crawling up my spine when I turned to face him. *I can't believe I was ever crazy about you,* I thought.

Frank frowned when he saw where I was pointing. "It's out of the way, but we can start there and jot down some descriptions of the atmosphere."

Frank started scribbling away the minute we sat down, smirking as he wrote. I opened up my notebook and stared down at the clean sheet of paper. Then I raised my gaze and peeked out at the dance floor, unable to resist looking at Paul. Why was I torturing myself like this? I'd blown it. He was in love with her. And we weren't even friends anymore.

"Do you think we should dance?" Frank asked.

"Huh?"

"Well, we'd get better material if we were out there with them."

I smiled weakly. There had been a time when I would have thought he was just making an excuse to dance with me.

He pushed his chair back and stood up. "So shall we?" he asked again.

I swallowed, trying to think of an excuse not to dance with him. There was no way I could be out there, in his arms but feeling *nothing,* surrounded by people who really cared about each other.

"We're undercover, remember? You don't want that crazy getup of yours to go to waste." He took my hand and led me to the dance floor.

Okay, I can do this, I told myself.

Frank put one arm around my waist and held my hand the way you danced with a relative or someone you had no feelings for romantically. *This would have killed me if I still liked him,* I realized, grateful I'd already seen the light.

We swayed with the music. I shut my eyes, pretending this wasn't Frank. It was someone I cared about, someone whose arms I *wanted* to feel around me. I sighed and tightened my grip around his neck, imagining that I was dancing with . . . *Paul.*

I opened my eyes and suddenly there he was. Paul. Right behind Frank, dancing with Katie and looking straight at me.

I let go of Frank and started backing away from him, bumping into a couple behind me. "I'm—I'm sorry," I stammered to them.

"What's the matter?" Frank asked.

"It's—uh, it's an inspiration," I blurted out. "I've got to go write." I hurried off the dance floor, weaving around couples.

I spotted my notebook, my only Valentine's Day offering, on the table. I snatched it up, then dashed through the exit door. The romantic song that had been blaring in the gym faded to a distant sound. I burst into tears as the double doors swung shut behind me.

I didn't know where to go, what to do. The one person who'd been comforting me since I was five was inside, dancing with the girl he loved. And there wouldn't be any comfort from Paul anymore—ever.

The gym door opened behind me and music blared out, a fast song. I wiped away my tears, embarrassed that anyone might see me crying on Valentine's Day. How pathetic would that be?

"Erica?"

Paul. He *was* talking to me.

I was afraid to turn around. Afraid that the second I focused in on all the worry and concern in his sweet, beautiful brown eyes, I'd burst into sobs again.

He stepped around me, standing directly in front of me. He lifted up my chin with his fingers. "What did that jerk do?" he demanded.

"Nothing," I mumbled, refusing to meet his gaze. "You were right about him all along," I choked out between sobs. "So go ahead and tell me 'I told you so.' I deserve it."

"I'm sorry," Paul said softly. "I never wanted you to get hurt. He's not worth your tears, Erica."

"He's not why I'm—" *Shut up, Erica. Just shut up. Paul doesn't need this dumped on him. He doesn't need to know how you feel about him. That'll just make him feel guilty for having to hurt you now that he loves Katie. If you really love him, you'll just shut up.*

"Then why?" Paul prodded. He dropped his hand, and I still couldn't look up at him. How could he still be so wonderful after the way I'd treated him in the *Postscript* office? He lifted my chin up again. "Erica? Will you look at me? Please. This is *me,* Paul."

Yeah, I know.

His touch was so soft and warm that my last shred of reserve dissolved and I burst into tears, my

163

body shaking as I sobbed. He wrapped his arms tightly around me and held me close against him, rocking me. I buried my face in his chest.

I needed him so badly, and I never wanted to let go of him. But I'd have to.

Finally the sobs began to subside, and Paul pulled back slightly, lifting my face up and wiping away the tears from my cheeks.

"It's okay," he murmured into my ear. "It's okay. Shh."

I finally met his gaze. I sucked in my breath and my hands began to tremble. I could see all the years of our friendship, our amazing friendship, reflected back in his soft, sensitive eyes.

My heart was hammering, and I could even hear his beating just as quickly. Still staring into his eyes, I inched closer to him. His face moved forward too, until there was so little space between us I could feel his breath on my cheek.

His lips were almost touching mine. Just another centimeter more and they would be pressed together. I could imagine the softness of his mouth, the sweetness of kissing him . . .

Omigod. My heart started to pound even harder. Everything about kissing Paul made sense . . . it made such total, *natural* sense. Paul's touch made sense, holding him made sense, being so near him made sense. Wanting to kiss him made sense.

I gulped.

Frank had never made me feel this way—no one had. I'd wanted to kiss Frank, yes, but no one but

Paul knew me inside and out and had the power to reach me when I was certain I couldn't be reached. Paul *was* my best friend.

And I'm in love with him.

Don't dump this on him. Don't do it. If you really love him, you won't. Not when he's found someone else. Someone he loves. He's just comforting you now—he doesn't love you back. Not anymore.

"I—I have to go," I stammered, backing away from him. He stared at me, confusion in those beautiful eyes. And then I ran.

WILL YOU BE MY VALENTINE?
A LESSON LEARNED TOO LATE
by Erica Park

"Valentine's Day is the best—it's the one day totally devoted to love."

That's just one of the responses I got when I interviewed some of you for this article. My questions
were designed to show all of you that Valentine's
Day is a ridiculous holiday, a contrived occasion
where people express superficial emotions through
corny, overly sentimental gifts.

I was wrong.

As I listened to what each of you shared, I realized
that it doesn't matter why Valentine's Day started or
how we choose to celebrate the day. It doesn't matter
if there are a million teddy bears out there clutching
heart-shaped boxes of chocolates in their paws. You
see, diamonds are valuable because they are precious
and rare—just like a true friend, or a person who
knows you inside and out. However, diamonds are
special also because they are *not* uncommon. Their
meaning is immediately understood to the recipi-
ent—a diamond engagement ring symbolizes love
and commitment because it's the traditional gift for a
promise of a life together.

This is also true for the kinds of presents given on
Valentine's Day. What do red roses, chocolate, and
adorable stuffed animals represent? They are a simple
and easy way to show someone how much you care,
just like a hand held under the table or a stolen kiss in

the hallway. Affectionate gestures like these and sentimental words that have been around forever, like "Be mine" or "You have my heart," are the symbols of what you feel inside. Just because they are not unique or original does not make them any less real or heartfelt. When you love someone, you show them in every way you can— whether it's handing that person your last token in the arcade, holding her when she's sad, or giving her a giant box of Whitman's truffles.

Who cares if the words on the card you got are written by Shakespeare or Hallmark? They mean the same thing to the person who gave you the card, and they should mean the same thing to you. I didn't understand this until recently, when I discovered what real love is. I learned that it's easy to make fun of mushy messages on the candygrams sent to you year after year—until the year when you don't get one. That's when you realize how warm it used to make you feel inside, and *why* it did. It's easy to talk about the silliness of couples who are affectionate with each other—until you actually feel strongly enough about someone to understand what it's like to want to hold that person and never let go.

Finally, it's easy to laugh at the silliness of Valentine's Day—until you see that Valentine's Day is about treasuring what you have, and, sometimes, about understanding what you've lost.

Fifteen

I BREATHED A sigh of relief when I entered the *Postscript* office on Tuesday morning. The Valentine's Day edition had been passed out in homeroom, and I was ready to face Frank. He'd left messages for me Saturday night and twice on Sunday, and I'd avoided him all day Monday. All I had to say to him was in my article, which I'd turned in directly to Mr. Serson the day before.

"So Ms. Anti-mush has a heart after all." Linda walked into the tiny office, grinning at me.

"Yeah, just in time to get it broken," I muttered. I glanced up at the doorway as a few other staffers strolled in, Frank included.

His own article on the evolving history of Valentine's Day had been really dry and boring. Just like him.

"What were you trying to do?" he asked, glaring at me as he slapped a *Postscript* on the desk.

I smiled at him. "Trying to do?" I echoed. "I don't understand." I folded my arms across my chest.

"With your *article*," he said, rolling his eyes. "What was all that sappy drivel about affection and commitment? I thought you were different. But obviously you and I have *nothing* in common. You must have known how I'd react when I read it. So I'll take that as a breakup."

Linda, David, and Carrie, all within hearing distance, shook their heads and rolled their eyes. Had I been the only one blind to what a total jerk he was?

"I never said you weren't smart, Frank." He frowned. "You're absolutely right," I continued. "And I'm glad we have nothing in common. I could never be as rude as you are. All you do is put people down. I'm just sorry I ever helped you with your campaign for the historian job. You could never represent our student body because you have no respect for any of us."

He gasped, staring at me.

"I love this paper," I continued. "And there's no way I'm giving up what I worked so hard for just because I have to work with you. But yes, you can definitely take my article as a breakup. It's so *cute* that you knew that already."

Frank smirked. "Whatever." He turned on his heel and sat down at his desk, his back to the room.

Linda rushed up to me. "Are you okay?"

I shrugged. "Just working on my editing skills." She frowned in puzzlement. "I was practicing how to make important cuts," I explained with my first smile since Saturday night.

I headed toward my locker after school, relieved to see that Linda and Sharon weren't around. They both kept pressing me about what was up with Frank and Paul. Linda had filled Sharon in on what happened with Frank that morning, and they were dying to know what had led up to it.

I just wasn't in the mood to explain. Frank had left three messages for me over the weekend, Paul zero. And he hadn't been in history Monday or that morning. I hadn't seen Katie around either. Maybe they were both working really hard to avoid me, which made sense.

I hadn't expected to hear from Paul after I ran away from the dance Saturday night; it had been Valentine's Day, and he belonged with Katie. They'd probably spent Sunday together too. At least Paul and I had sort of made up that night. At least he didn't hate me anymore. But I figured he still thought taking a break was a good idea.

I swung open my locker and shoved my books inside, surprised to see a folded piece of paper on the top shelf. *What's this?* I wondered, plucking it out. My name was written on the folded side in handwriting I knew as well as my own. *Paul's.*

I swallowed hard, slowly opening the loose-leaf paper.

Erica, meet me after school at Ms. Pac-Man.

I scanned the one-line note again, making sure

I'd read it correctly. Why would Paul ask me to meet him at the Ms. Pac-Man machine? That video game hadn't worked in six months, and everyone at the Bowl-a-Rama insisted they weren't fixing it.

Maybe he figured a quiet corner of the arcade room was perfect for telling me we couldn't be friends anymore. That our broken friendship couldn't be repaired. And the Bowl-a-Rama, the place we'd spent so much time in over the past nine years, was probably the sweetest place he could think of to say good-bye.

I took a deep breath, then pulled open the door to the arcade room in the Bowl-a-Rama.

I staggered backward.

Paul sat at a cloth-covered table in the center of the room, surrounded by flowers, balloons, streamers, and red boxes of candy. A boom box was propped on the old Space Invaders machine; a romantic song played softly.

"Happy belated Valentine's Day," he said when I'd finally turned to stare at him.

"I don't understand," I squeaked out.

"Lee helped me set it all up." Paul grinned. "Here," he added, holding out a candygram.

I sucked in my breath and took it, opening the little note attached.

Dear Erica,
  I'll make it simple this year. You mean everything, and you always will. There

aren't enough chocolates or flowers in the world to symbolize how in love with you I am, but here's a start.

Love, Paul

My hands trembled and I stared up at him. "But Katie . . . ," I began.

"Katie broke up with me on Valentine's Day morning," Paul explained. "I asked her if she'd mind stopping at the comics convention for even twenty minutes, and she totally lost it. She said that was the *last* place she'd ever want to go, especially on Valentine's Day."

My mouth dropped open. "And then," he continued, "she told me she had a feeling the real reason I wanted to go was because *you* were there, even though you'd be with Frank. And she was right, but I didn't tell her that."

"She must be so upset," I managed to croak out. The shock of everything I'd just heard had me frozen in place.

"Nope," he said. "She told me she really liked me as a friend, but that she didn't think I was right for her, that we had nothing in common."

"But you two went to the dance together," I said. "I *saw* you slow-dancing."

"We went as friends," Paul replied, standing up and stepping closer to me. "There are definitely no hard feelings on either side. Plus neither of us could get another date that fast." He grinned, moving even closer to me.

"If only I'd known that night!" I exclaimed.

"I'm glad you didn't. Otherwise you might not have written that article in that same way. Straight from the heart."

He took my hands in his.

"So you know, then," I said. "About how I feel, that I wrote it about us. I mean, about *me* and—well, about what I—" I took a deep breath.

"Maybe you should say it directly, just so there won't be any confusion," he suggested.

"I love you, Paul," I said. "I've fallen very much in love with you. Totally, old-fashionedly in love with you."

He stared at me. "Say something!" I burst out.

A huge grin spread across his face, and his eyes gleamed brightly.

"Like what?" he asked. "The girl I've wanted my entire life has just confessed to being *madly* in love with me. What's the correct response?"

I burst out laughing.

"Erica," he said softly, "I could never do anything *but* love you. That's why I told you to meet me by Ms. Pac-Man. What we have could never, ever be broken."

My whole body seemed to melt at his words. "I was so afraid I'd lost you," I choked out. "I have so much to tell you, so much about what I learned, what I realized—"

"Shh," Paul whispered, touching his fingers to my lips. I blinked as a tingly sensation raced all the way down to my toes. Then he wrapped both arms

174

around me, pulling me against him. "We have all the time in the world for that," he said.

I leaned my head on his broad chest, sighing as his arms tightened around me. We swayed to the music. I raised my chin, and he tilted his down.

For the first time in nine years, we kissed. Really kissed.

We held each other so tightly I was sure we would blend into one person. I savored the perfection, the absolute *rightness* of the moment. Tears of pure happiness built up in my eyes.

The kiss seemed to last an eternity, but eventually we pulled back, our eyes and arms still locked together.

"Was it worth the wait?" I joked, surprised to hear the trembling in my voice.

Paul smiled, then nodded. "I love you," he whispered.

And then he leaned down and kissed me again, gently and easily. The feel of him was both familiar and new, as though I'd just found something I'd been missing for years.

TOP TEN REASONS TO BE IN LOVE
by Erica Park, for her private journal

10. The constant candygrams, even though Valentine's Day is, like, 360 days away.
9. Kisses in the hallways at school.
8. History class is a lot more exciting.
7. Sharon and Linda and I can talk about it for hours and never get bored.
6. You can go on sap-filled double dates with people like Katie and her new boyfriend, David, the *Postscript* design staffer.
5. Studying together makes it go faster.
4. Someone always saves you a seat at lunch.
3. You don't need Drab Days because every day is incredible.
2. Love is just amazing.
1. You can celebrate your boyfriend's winning the post of school historian in the most romantic way possible: bowling, skee ball, and a double order of fries with extra Old Bay seasoning.

Do you ever wonder about falling in love? About members of the opposite sex? Do you need a little friendly advice but have no one to turn to? Well, that's where we come in . . . Jenny and Jake. Send us those questions you're dying to ask, and we'll give you the straight scoop on life and love.

DEAR JAKE

Q: *A friend gave a boy (her friend) my e-mail address, and we've gotten to know each other online. We've written each other almost every day for the past few weeks, and our conversations are always interesting and fun. We haven't met in person (neither of us has brought that up), but we did talk on the phone once a couple of weeks ago. Well, he hasn't called me since then, and we're still only in contact through e-mail. I really like him, but I'm beginning to wonder if we're ever going to talk on the phone and even meet in person—or if all he wants us to be is pen pals. I'm tempted to stop e-mailing him—maybe then he'll call me. Do you think this is a good idea?*

MK, Dover, DE

A: It could work, but it could also backfire. He might think you stopped responding to his e-mail because you're not interested in him anymore. That might make him just give up and stop writing to you too. How about a direct approach? If you really want this relationship to go somewhere outside of cyberspace, why don't you come right out and suggest that the two of you turn off your computers and start talking on the phone? If he's not comfortable with that, it doesn't mean he'll never be. He just might need more time to get to know you through e-mail.

Q: *The guy I like is going out with my best friend. They both know I like him—actually, everyone in school knows! Recently he told me that if he and my friend break up, he'll go out with me. A couple of days later we ran into each other at a friend's house, and one thing led to another . . . and he kissed me. Should I tell my friend what happened, or should I just forget it and make sure it never happens again?*

RL, Pensacola, FL

A: This is a very sticky situation. I do suggest that you tell your friend what happened (especially before she hears it from someone else). She knows you like him, so she's probably going to feel betrayed by you and by him. Sounds to me as though your friend and her boyfriend need to talk and settle things between them. And then you and your friend need to do the same. If they do break up over this, I don't recommend trying to fill her shoes right away. You just might lose her as a friend for good.

DEAR JENNY

Q: *Chris and I have been friends for a long time, and I like him a lot. We flirt with each other, and he's always saying really sweet things to me, but we've never been anything more than friends. Everyone thinks we should be dating, but I don't want to ruin the friendship. I'm afraid that if we start going out and then break up, things will be different. What should I do?*

LW, Warren, MI

A: You'd be surprised to know how many letters I receive from girls and guys who have the same question you do! If both of you are bursting to kiss each other, then I say go for it. After all, the two of you already share one of the most important aspects of a romance: friendship. Worrying about what will happen to the friendship if the romance doesn't work out is valid. But it all boils down to the fact that you'll never know unless you try. Even if you decide not to try, the two of you just might find it's impossible to ignore your romantic feelings for each other!

Q: *I have a really big problem. I am totally in love with my sister's boyfriend. I don't mean that I have a crush on him—I'm saying I am absolutely head-over-heels in love. I am so happy when he's around and miserable when he's not. I'm torn between feeling guilty for having these feelings and wanting to tell the world—my* *sister included—how I feel. It's getting harder and harder to keep my feelings for him to myself. Should I just suffer in silence and hope I'll get over him one day, or do I dare tell him how I feel?*

TK, Richmond, VA

A: Being in love with someone you can't have is really painful. But when that someone is your sister's boyfriend, there's only one thing to do, in my opinion: keep your feelings to yourself, your journal, your best friend. Is your relationship with your sister worth risking over a romantic relationship? I doubt it. I know it's hard to deny your feelings, but just remember that the guy you want is taken—and taken by your own sister. That makes him doubly off-limits!

Do you have any questions about love?
Although we can't respond individually to your letters,
you just might find your questions answered in our column.
Write to:
Jenny Burgess or Jake Korman
c/o 17th Street Productions, Inc.
33 West 17th Street
New York, NY 10011

Don't miss any of the books in *Love Stories*
—the romantic series from Bantam Books!

You'll always remember your first love.

Love Stories

Looking for signs he's ready to fall in love?

Want the guy's point of view?

Then you should check out *Love Stories*. Romantic stories that tell it like it is—why he doesn't call, how to ask him out, when to say good-bye.

Love Stories
Available wherever books are sold.